A**MOTOR**NOVEL

SATURDAY NIGHT DIRT

SATURDAY NIGHT DIRT

BY WILL WEAVER

SQUARE
FISH

FARRAR, STRAUS AND GIROUX

SQUARE
FISH

An imprint of Macmillan

SATURDAY NIGHT DIRT. Copyright © 2008 by Will Weaver.
All rights reserved. Printed in June 2010 in the United States of America
by R. R. Donnelley & Sons Company, Harrisonburg, Virginia.
For information, address Square Fish, 175 Fifth Avenue, New York, NY 10010.

Square Fish and the Square Fish logo are trademarks of Macmillan
and are used by Farrar, Straus and Giroux under license from Macmillan.

Library of Congress Cataloging-in-Publication Data
Weaver, Will.
    Saturday night dirt / Will Weaver.
        p.   cm.
    Summary: In a small town in northern Minnesota, the much-
anticipated Saturday night dirt-track race at the old-fashioned, barely
viable Headwaters Speedway becomes, in many ways, an important
life-changing event for all the participants on and off the track.
    ISBN: 978-0-312-56131-4
    [1. Automobile racing—Fiction.   2. Stock car racing—Fiction.
3. Interpersonal relations—Fiction.   4. Minnesota—Fiction.]
    I. Title.

PZ7.W3623Sat 2008
[Fic]—dc22

                                                          2007006988

Originally published in the United States by Farrar, Straus and Giroux
Designed by Jonathan Bartlett
Square Fish logo designed by Filomena Tuosto
First Square First Edition: 2009
10   9   8   7   6   5   4   3
www.squarefishbooks.com

SPECIAL THANKS

to Northwest Technical College, Bemidji, Minnesota, and all the guys in the High Performance Automotive Machinist Program: Paul Nelson (instructor), Mike Langerman, Rich Batt, Mike Clough, Kyle Sparby, Dan Koetz, Cody Hansen, Eddie Driscoll, Dallas Grübe, Matthew Bonebrake, Ken Hodgden, Todd Wurgler, and others. I thought I knew something about cars until I spent a year in the shop with you.

Thanks also to my crew chief, Bill Smith, for all your work on our red and black No. 16 Modified. Thanks as well to Quinn Schreiber, chassis builder, and Brian and Mary Strand at FastLane.

Thanks, finally, to Bemidji Speedway and others like it across America for their dedication to grassroots auto racing.

Saturday

NOON

TRACE

"Torque wrench."

Trace Bonham, seventeen, short and stocky with un-smiling brown eyes, turned to the big toolbox on wheels. He yanked open drawer 5—all screwdrivers—then drawer 4—all sockets.

"Come on, kid. Bottom drawer, left side," Larry Rawlins barked. He was the unofficial crew chief on the Bonham Farms yellow No. 32 Street Stock, a 1986 Monte Carlo. Street Stock, as a class, meant a full-framed American car with only minor modifications. It was one of the last car classes before racing—engines especially—got really expensive. Larry was bent over the engine compartment. Freshened cylinder heads for the 350-cubic-inch Chevrolet block were finally in place. Tonight, maybe the Chevy would run right.

Trace kept looking. "More like middle drawer, right

side," he finally said. He turned and slapped the heavy dial-gauge wrench onto Larry's grimy palm.

"If you had to thrash this car yourself, you'd know where everything was," Larry said, handing Trace the speed wrench in return. "It might even make you a better driver."

"I'd be a better driver if I had some top-end horse-power," Trace muttered.

Larry, a thick-necked guy wearing a stained seed cap, didn't answer. He didn't hear well—too many years around high-rpm equipment. Most of the week he drove farm equipment or grain trucks for Trace's dad—deeper in the hangar-size shed were Don Bonham's combines and tractors—but Saturdays he worked on the Bonham stock car. Saturday night was dirt-track racing.

"Take me, I had to work my way up," Larry began.

"Listen!" Trace shot back, loudly this time. "I can't help it if my old man likes racing and wants me to drive. That's just the way it is, all right?"

"Hey, kid, don't get your shorts in a wad!" Larry said, straightening up. "Save that for tonight."

At that moment the shop door banged open, and Trace's dad hustled in. Don Bonham, stocky and strong like Trace, had salt-and-pepper hair cropped short and a very tanned face. He never made quiet entrances. As he stalked across the shop, his cowboy boots went *pock-pock-pock* on the concrete floor.

"Hey, boss," Larry said, with chew-speckled teeth; he was always cheerful when Trace's dad came around.

Nodding briefly to his son and Larry, Don bent over the engine compartment. He stared. "Looks like you got a ways to go."

"No problem," Larry said. "I should have it running by three o'clock or so."

"I hope," Don said. "We got racing tonight."

"If it don't rain," Larry said, not moving any faster. "Sixty percent chance, they say."

Don pursed his lips. "I heard forty to fifty percent."

"No matter, we'll be ready," Larry added cheerfully. He was the kind of guy who knew just how far to push things, a trait about him that drove Trace crazy.

Don jerked his chin toward his son. "Trace been any help so far?"

"Couldn't do without him," Larry said with an exaggerated drawl—and a sly glance to Don.

Don did not smile; he was not a smiling kind of guy. "Well, kick his butt if he doesn't," Don said. He winked at Trace.

Larry glanced at Trace. "He probably thinks I couldn't." Trace was silent. *Bring it on.*

"None of that, boys," Don said. "We're a team here—we all got to get along."

"Just trying to teach him everything I know, boss," Larry said as he leaned into his torque wrench.

"I learned that in the first five minutes," Trace murmured.

His father shot Trace a frown. "Anyway, let's keep doin' it, Larry," Don said loudly. "The clock is ticking." As Larry fit the socket onto the next head bolt and made an exaggerated wrenching motion with his stubby, muscular arms, Don looked at Trace and nodded toward the door.

Outside, Trace squinted in the bright sunshine glinting off metal sheds and galvanized grain bins. The cloudless sky was a big blue oven holding in the July heat and humidity—or maybe it was his red-flushed face that gave off the sweaty warmth.

"Everything going all right in there?" his father asked, closing the door behind them. He put on his wraparound sunglasses. Trace's dad was a farmer who never wore a seed cap, and always carried a BlackBerry. He used it to keep track of his farm business plus all the latest racing news.

"Larry," Trace said with a shrug. "You know him. Likes to make himself indispensable. Create emergencies where there shouldn't be any. Those heads should have been on yesterday—so we can figure out where we're losing horsepower."

His father paused. "Larry says the motor runs fine."

"It doesn't run fine," Trace said. "I keep telling you that."

"Well, he'll get it figured out. Bear with him," Don said. "Larry's a useful employee."

Trace rolled his eyes.

"I'm serious, Son," his dad replied. "There's a place for guys like him—men to do the heavy lifting, the grunt work of life. Some people are born on the long end of the wrench, others on the short end, if you know what I mean—"

"Yeah, yeah," Trace said, cutting him off. "I'm just saying, when it comes to engine and setup work, I can do everything he can in half the time. And I *like* working on the car."

"You're a driver, Trace, not a mechanic."

Trace glanced away.

"Unless you don't want to drive," his father added.

"I want to drive," Trace said sharply.

"There are plenty of kids out there looking for a ride."

"I *said* I want to drive."

"But do you want to win?"

"Yes, I want to win! If you don't think so, drive the car yourself," Trace shot back.

His father smiled for the first time. "That's the spirit. I want you to get mad out there tonight—bump some people, run some people off the road."

Trace kicked at the gravel and did not reply.

"Anyway, I'm too old to drive," his father said. "Climbing through a stock car window is a young man's game. Hurts my back just watching you."

Trace shrugged. His father had a way of doing that to him. Jerking him around. Playing him like a puppet on short strings.

"Plus I just happen to like watching my son go flat out on Saturday night dirt," his father added.

Trace allowed his father to give him a brief, one-armed hug.

"I wonder if that orange No. 27 from Grand Rapids will show up tonight," his father said, glancing at his

BlackBerry. "The guy who beat you down low in turn 3 on that last feature?"

It wasn't like Trace needed this jab from his father to relive that humiliation: He'd been running fourth with the pedal down, straining for just a few more rpm. Orange No. 27 was looming larger and larger in the roaring dust off his right side—then, in turn 3, no more orange. Trace knew better than to look back but swiveled his head over his right shoulder. Gone! No orange anywhere. He must have spun out. That meant fourth place and at least some points for yellow No. 32. That, and maybe a break from his old man. Suddenly orange No. 27 sharked in low and tight on Trace's left side. A screech of tin on tin as he and Trace locked up. For a long second the two cars were welded together. Trace pressed the pedal so hard his leg started to cramp—he tried to pinch the orange car and take away his line—but there was no more horsepower. Orange No. 27 shrugged loose from Trace and steadily pulled away. Trace faded to sixth place.

"Really?" Trace said sarcastically. "I'd totally forgotten." He could feel the heat, the anger, in his face.

His dad stepped back to take full measure of his son, then nodded approval. "I think we're gonna have a good night of racing. Now head back in there and help Larry get that beast running."

"Running is one thing, running right's another," Trace said, but his father was already walking away. Trace stared after him, then headed back to the shop. On the way, he squinted again at the sky: a few wispy clouds in the west, but no real weather in sight. Sixty percent chance of rain—yeah, right, Larry. At the shop door, he paused to take a breath, and to remind himself of one fact: tonight, win, lose, or break, at least he'd get to see Mel Walters. ·

MELODY

Melody (Mel) Walters, seventeen, kicked dirt. She wore dusty running shoes and had tanned legs and arms; a blond ponytail poked through the back of her World of Outlaws cap. She and her father, Johnny Walters, were inspecting turn 1 at Headwaters Speedway. George, their dirt man, had graded the quarter-mile dirt oval the evening before, but there was still a soft spot. Soft spots turned into ruts. Ruts broke axles and tie-rods. "The last thing we need is for some car to throw a wheel into the stands and hurt somebody," she said.

"I'll get him to pack it some more," her father said from behind her. As usual, he remained on his ATV.

"It needs water, too," Mel said, glancing over her shoulder at him. His forearms were massive from rolling his wheelchair, and he swung a tanned hand down to gather some dirt. Mel knelt down and scraped up her own handful—during the summer racing season she stopped worrying about her fingernails. The dull-brown clay mix did not gum up between her fingers. It should have squeezed into a ball, like kindergarten Play-Doh. This dirt was more like cornflake dust at the bottom of the box. "George should have watered the track last night, not five hours before hot laps," Mel said. Across in the pit area, George was only now filling the tanker truck.

"He thought it would rain last night," her father said, letting the dusty mix sift through his fingers.

"Don't say *that* word," Mel replied. Another rained-out Saturday night or two and none of this would matter. Headwaters Speedway would be in serious trouble at the bank. That was her main goal this summer: to keep the speedway afloat. Her dad had no idea how bad things were.

At the sudden chirp and whistle, she glanced up at the ospreys. Every summer the same stupid pair of birds raised their chicks atop the middle light pole in the speedway infield.

"Dinner is served," her dad said, looking up through his mirrored sunglasses. His salt-and-pepper ponytail swung as he turned.

"Fish again?" Mel asked sarcastically. An incoming osprey clutched a skinny northern pike torpedo-style under its belly. The chicks cheeped insanely and pushed their furry heads upward from the nest. The wagon wheel of halogen bulbs on the light pole was almost buried under a thick donut of sticks and reedy trash. "Someday that nest is going to catch on fire," Mel said, vaulting onto the back of the four-wheeler. "Then we'll have to pay for new lights, a new pole, and a cherry-picker truck to put it up."

Johnny watched the birds. "Honey, you worry too much," he answered. "If it happens, it happens. Besides, race fans like the birds. What other speedway has its own osprey nest?"

"Yeah, yeah," Mel muttered, hooking her arms loosely around her dad's waist—then poking his ribs to get him going. "Somebody's got to worry about things around here."

"Which is why I had you, baby!" her dad tossed over his shoulder, and then he accelerated the mud-spattered Bombardier.

Mel clenched both arms around her dad's waist but thought of her mother, who lived in Ohio. Only a woman could "have" a kid, but she didn't call her father on that tiny little fact. She hated her mother too much. Her mother had left her father hardly a year after his sprint car accident—when Melody was eight years old and still called Melody. "I just can't deal with a husband in a wheelchair," she announced one day.

Well, good for you—what can you deal with? On bad days, like this one was shaping up to be, Mel had silent conversations with her mother—dialogues that always ended in screaming matches.

As her father drove the banked clay into turn 2, she held on tighter. She wished she could have seen him race more often. As a kid, she took his racing for granted. Loud cars, each with a shiny rooftop wing, were part of her life, and she expected they always would be. So she didn't pay attention. Didn't watch the way she should have. Mainly, she remembered the accident: The slow-motion flipping, his No. 14a sprint car's rooftop spoiler tearing loose, then flying like a kite above the tangle of cars, her father's ride suspended upside down, his arms loose out the cockpit, flapping as if he was trying to fly the car, trying to land it upright. She wasn't there at Knoxville, Iowa, when it happened; a professional photographer caught the crash. His photos made the cover of *Open Wheel* magazine. There was an amateur videotape version of it in one of those horrible "Worst of ———" video collections of fatal racing crashes—as if she would ever watch that. The still photos were bad enough. All she knew about the accident was that a young driver from Pennsylvania was killed, and two other drivers, including her father, badly injured. That was enough.

The shrieks of the ospreys broke through her thoughts. The arriving male—slightly bigger—circled the nest to show off his catch. The female hopped onto the rim of the nest, where she flapped her wings and whistled again and again. As the male touched down, his mate launched for some sky time, some hunting time of her own. It was a dumb location for a nest, but they made a great team.

Mel's father stopped in turn 2 to watch the birds. "One thousand one, one thousand two," he began. On "three," the departing bird let loose a long white strand of poop.

"Plus they're dirty!" Mel said into her father's ear. "It's not like we need more you-know-what to deal with around here."

"Hey, everybody in the infield knows better than to park beneath the osprey nest," Johnny said.

JOHNNY

Johnny Walters, forty-five, former sprint car driver, worried about Melody. Melody and the weather, in that order. There was a chance of rain tonight, and that he couldn't control. His daughter was his daily worry. She worked too hard—took too much responsibility for speedway operations. Making her "track manager" last summer on her sixteenth birthday, presenting her with an engraved name tag, was a mostly a joke. An honorary title. No way he could afford a real track manager.

In northern Minnesota, Headwaters Speedway was a dusty dirt circle track with wooden bleachers and three and a half employees (he was the half-man). Melody did anything and everything—from nailing a loose board in the grandstand to advertising and payroll. George Huff took care of the actual track, the infield, and the pit area. A bunch of volunteers filled in the rest of the slots. Art Lempola did the announcing. His wife and two other ladies worked the booth with him, keeping track of cars along with Maurice Battier, the flagman. Four volunteer "spotters" talked to Maurice, the pit steward, and Melody through their radio headsets. The spotters helped the steward confirm car order on restarts. Modern tracks used radio-controlled transponders, one for each car, and a digital leaderboard for the fans. Headwaters was old-school and then some. Two white-haired ladies worked the main gate ticket booth. Without the volunteers—bless them, every one—Headwaters Speedway could not have survived.

"Two looks good, let's check turn 3," Mel said, swinging herself onto the rear. Johnny nodded and accelerated down the straightaway.

Situated between Duluth and Grand Forks, and four hours north of Minneapolis, Headwaters Speedway sat on the fringe of racing country. Dirt-track racing was more popular in southern Minnesota, Wisconsin, and Iowa—even North Dakota. Good dirt racing was coming, drafting in the widening reach of NASCAR, but it wasn't here yet. Headwaters was not set up for sprint cars, plus it did not draw the big-name Super Stocks, Modifieds, and Late Models—the touring teams that would pull in bigger crowds. On some nights, Headwaters drew only a half dozen Late Models, which was barely enough to make a race. Johnny was thinking of dropping Late Models and focusing more on local Hobby Stocks and amateur racers—perhaps adding demolition derbies—but Melody was against it. She had always taken the racetrack seriously, maybe more seriously than he did. The speedway was her life; she would sleep nights in the announcer's booth if he allowed it. It wasn't healthy.

"Are any of your friends from town coming out to the races tonight?" he asked over his shoulder.

"I doubt it," she said. "Anyway, it's not like I have time for them on race night."

"Maybe if you gave them some comp tickets—"

"Like we can afford comp tickets?" she interrupted.

Johnny slowed at turn 3. Then he said, "How about that Hafner boy, that kid in your grade who used to call you? Does he ever come to the races?"

"He's not that into cars," Melody said sarcastically.

"I'd be into cars—if I knew you were."

"Stop it, Dad," Melody said. "You have to like me—you're my father."

"Or that grounds guy I hired, Pat, the one who's in band and choir with you. He's a nice kid." Every summer Johnny hired a kid to mow lawn, clean the grounds, and park cars on race nights. This time he'd chosen a nice-looking, upstanding boy from town, a kid in the same grade as Melody. He was all the more useful because he could sing the national anthem.

"He doesn't know a spark plug from a lightbulb," Melody said, ending that discussion.

"What about Trace Bonham? You used to see him once in a while," Johnny said, braking.

"Yeah, but then he got serious about being a race car driver," Melody said.

Johnny didn't reply. He came to a full stop.

"Sorry," Melody said. "I didn't mean anything." She hugged him briefly, then hopped off the four-wheeler.

Johnny watched her walk the turn, briskly, head down, eyes on the dirt. He glanced skyward. The weather was sunny, though some light cumulus was building in the west.

Melody knelt and felt the dirt. Took up a handful and smelled it.

Johnny looked at the sky once more. Maybe if they got rained out again, it would be a sign, a message. Sell this place and do something else. At least his daughter could have a normal life.

GEORGE

The man who ran the track's road grader and water truck was George Huff. He was sixty-two but looked eighty-two, a stooped, dusty man in tattered coveralls. His responsibility included the dirt track itself, the center infield, and the pit area. Pit row was located on the north side of the oval track. Bigger speedways staged everything— their tractors, graders, water trucks, tow trucks, race cars, crews, and ambulances—in the center infield. With a quarter-mile oval, there wasn't enough room.

The infield at Headwaters held only the essentials.

Near the center was the scale shack and drive-across scale, where winning cars were checked against class weight limits. Nearby, directly across from the grandstand, was the winner's "circle," a space of concrete painted to look like a checkered flag. Here drivers received trophies and got their pictures taken against a low backdrop of billboards. At the base of each turn were bumper tires—heavy, scarred, log-skidder tires donated by local loggers, then painted white by you know who. The tires always needed rearranging—nudging with a tow truck—after a race. George couldn't keep up with it all.

Right now he sucked on a cigarette while he waited for the tanker to fill. Water pressure from the pit-area well was down a little more each week. His garden hose was cold and full but slow. The well needed a new submersible pump, but that meant pulling the pipe, something he could not do by himself. He hated to break the bad news to Mel and Johnny because they needed only good news these days. The old Ford truck that carried the water tank needed motor work, though he planned to nurse it through the rest of the summer, then freshen the engine this winter on his own time. Mel and Johnny didn't have to know.

"George?" Mel's voice crackled in his headset.

"I'm on it," he replied. "Truck is almost full."

"Thank you, George," Mel said cheerfully.

George would have watered the track yesterday, but the heat and humidity had made conditions ripe for a thunderstorm. A half inch of rain would have been perfect. It would have saved one more hour on the truck's engine. But the front was slow in coming, and no weather had materialized—not yet, anyway. He glanced at the sky, then across the track. In turn 4, Mel held up a handful of dirt to Johnny.

"I said I'm on it," George muttered.

PATRICK

Patrick Fletcher (he never went by Pat), seventeen, was already thinking about what to wear to work at the speedway. He had a full hour before he punched in at 2:00 p.m., but the choice of jeans was no easy matter. Not that people arriving at the Headwaters gate paid much attention to a parking lot guy's jeans, but there was always a chance that Mel Walters would come by on her four-wheeler.

Come by and notice him. Speak to him even. They talked occasionally at high school during choir or band, and briefly in the hallway, where she always drew a crowd. But at the speedway she was a different person. Busy. Distracted. Always talking into her headset or her cell phone. Being two places at once. The less time she had for him, the more he thought of her—even dreamed of her.

And what shoes to wear? Black Nikes or cowboy boots? Boots and jeans always went well together, but he felt false wearing cowboy boots. His parents were teachers, and he lived in town. What gave him the right to wear cowboy boots? Guys like Trace Bonham wore boots like a second skin; nobody would comment about Trace wearing boots.

Still, cowboy boots made him look taller (Patrick was five feet ten and, he hoped, still growing), plus Johnny Walters always wore cowboy boots. Then again, Johnny had been a race car driver and now owned the speedway; he had the authority to wear cowboy boots. Patrick was a junior-to-be, a high school music and choir geek who drove his parents' minivan to work (he hoped Mel wouldn't see him arrive). It was a mystery why Johnny Walters had hired him, but he was happy for the job, for the hours—if only he could figure out what to wear.

Plus there was the weather. If he wore boots tonight and it rained, they'd be ruined by the mud. He pointed the television remote and found the Weather Channel. A green smudge, like a giant thumbprint, lay west of Fargo, but there was no serious weather in Minnesota.

Maybe the cowboy boots after all.

MAURICE

Maurice Battier, fifty-nine, was the flagman at Headwaters Speedway. Right now he was at home standing in his skivvies before an ironing board. He was ironing and watching an old dirt-track racing movie with Mickey Rooney, *The Big Wheel*. He could stand around in his skivvies and watch movies because he lived alone, had never married. *Skivvies*, a word meaning underwear, was a term he'd learned in the Navy, where he had also learned how to wash and press his dress whites and his signal flags. A farm boy, he had never known what clean was until he joined the Navy. There he discovered that he liked clean— no more smelly cow barns and calf pens for him. He had stayed in the Navy for twenty-five years.

Maurice paused, iron suspended over a pant leg and its sharp white crease, to watch the flagman in the movie. In the old days, flagmen dressed up in suits and stood on the track—right on the dirt—as the cars whizzed by. Mickey Rooney, leading the pack in an open-cockpit car with tall spoke wheels, sped past, an arm's length from the flagman. The flagman held his ground like a matador in a bullring. Clouds of dust rolled over him. He had a decent figure-eight sweeping motion, though he did not make effective use of his upper body or point well. The best flagmen leaned sharply toward a passing car and jabbed their rolled-up flags at the offending driver like a teacher with a long ruler. Like a maestro at a symphony. Drivers needed to know that the flagman was in charge. Good flagmen— clearly this one was an actor—were hard to find.

Maurice had never planned to be a flagman. After his retirement, he did small Sheetrocking jobs (he liked Sheetrock because it was white and straight). He also kept the tidiest yard and flower beds in town, and went to the races on Saturday night. He ate his supper at Ritchie's BBQ Waggin. It was something he looked forward to all week.

Later, in the stands, he watched the people and listened in on their conversations. Saturday nights at the speedway were enjoyable—except for the local flagman. He was sloppily dressed, indecisive, and (Maurice's theory) color-blind. One night, after several confusing restarts, Maurice surprised himself by marching up to the announcer's booth and asking to speak to the owner. "You need a new flagman," he said.

The owner looked him up and down. Maurice was tidy and clean-shaven, as always.

"I was a signalman, first class, in the Navy," Maurice added.

"You're hired," the owner said.

Over the years, Maurice had worked for five track owners at Headwaters Speedway. Johnny Walters was the latest and to date the unluckiest. Johnny and his daughter, Mel, had more bad luck than the Navy had salt water. The father-daughter pair could pull a Saturday night thunderstorm down from Canada just by unlocking the speedway gates.

Maurice took no pay, and didn't ask about finances, but he had a bad feeling about this summer. What if the speedway went belly-up? What if it closed for good? What would he do, where would he go on Saturday nights? He put that thought out of his head and concentrated on his ironing. He pressed sharp creases in his white pants. After them, he turned to his flags. He laid them out: white, yellow, green, red, black, blue and yellow, checkered. He ironed them before every race.

BEAU

Beau Kim, formerly Beau Kim Carlson, was sixteen. Right now he was doing tai chi in his parents' garage. He knew about half the moves and made up the rest as he went along. After all, the tai chi was not for his health. At five feet, five inches, he was wiry and cut, a wrestler in the 123-pound class. He did tai chi for his car. For good luck tonight at the races. His ratty little Mod-Four, the pink and black No. 19z, took up one bay of the garage. Make that most of one bay. Mod-Fours were compact, four-cylinder race cars—not Midgets, which was a class by itself, but still short and boxy. At 1500 pounds, they weighed half as much as a Street Stock like Trace Bonham's. The rest of Beau's part of the garage was filled with his big red toolbox on wheels, a stack of rims and worn Hoosier tires, plus various spare parts, all from the local auto salvage yard. The car itself was held together by its reworked chassis, a homemade roll cage, two after-school jobs, and lots of charm.

He called it his "stone soup car." He had rescued the chassis from a wrecked Mod-Four over in Brainerd. The 2.3-liter engine came from a wrecked 1986 Ford Ranger. His tires, Hoosier Dirt Stocker A-60 × 13 size, had been scrounged, one here, one there, from other racing teams. Teams with sponsors threw away tires with several shows left in them. Every sponsored team had cast-off equipment, stuff they were not using. Beau was not shy about asking for it—plus it helped that he looked like some kind of orphan kid. That part made him feel cheap on occasion, but the ends justified the means. At sixteen, he owned his own race car: engine, tube chassis, aluminum driver's seat, seat belt and shoulder harness, lift-off steering wheel, roll cage, and riveted tin sides all the way around.

So his engine burned a quart of oil every race night and left a fine blue plume of smoke behind? Johnny Walters should pay him for fogging mosquitoes. Oil was cheaper than new piston rings, and No. 19z was still zippy enough to compete at the local level.

The best thing about No. 19z was its paint job: pink on black, with a pink stripe painted to look like a satin ribbon that tied in a three-dimensional bow on top of the car. The bow (Beau) part was a little too subtle for most race fans, but his friends all dug it. Now, at midsummer, Beau was fourth in points standing in the Mod-Four class at Headwaters. A win tonight would move him into second place, just behind Amber Jenkins and her red No. 13a.

Her very name shrank his happy place. He shook his

head to ward off her bad vibe—she was a totally annoying person—then finished his tai chi ritual with a low, extended bow to No. 19z and to the dirt-track gods. The side garage door opened. His mother, Linda Carlson, poked her head inside.

"Hey, Mom," he said, holding his pose. The doorway was directly behind him, but he could tell it was his mom because she didn't speak. "Is there something?" he added cheerfully.

"Your lunch is still warm, dear."

"Thanks, I'll be right there," Beau said. "Almost done here."

His mother made no departing sounds.

"What?" Beau said.

"Nothing. Well, not nothing. It makes me nervous when you do that."

"Do what?"

"That."

"You know what it's called. Tai chi. My own kind, that is."

"I know, I know. But it feels to me like some sort of religious thing."

Beau counted down—an effective bow needed at least sixty seconds (not that he was superstitious). Moving only his lips, he said, "It is and it isn't religious."

"You see? That's what worries me."

"Mom! It's mainly for good luck."

"Still," she said, "what would Pastor Atkinson say?"

"We could ask him."

His mother was silent.

"Tomorrow, after church, we'll ask him his position on tai chi," Beau said.

"Now you're making fun of me," his mother said. Her voice turned down at the end.

Beau broke his pose and looked her way. She was a short, pudgy, round-eyed, very pale-faced, very excellent mom. "No, Ma," he said. "You just worry too much."

She pursed her lips and frowned. "Your father and I, we had no trouble with you taking back your birth name. I mean, that happens nowadays with, you know . . ."

"Adopted kids?" Beau said easily.

"Yes," she went on quickly. "But we do worry that you might be losing your religion, too." Her face scrunched up, and her eyes glistened.

"I'm fine, Mom. Really," Beau said, and hurried forward to give her a hug. "Stop worrying, all right?"

"Okay. I'll try," she said, clutching him tight around his ribs — holding him as if he were going away forever.

"What's for lunch?" Beau asked, breaking free.

"Your favorite — macaroni and cheese."

"Great," he said, following her inside — into the kitchen of this American rambler home with his Caucasian, Lutheran mother. He kept having weird thoughts like that lately. Like what his real mother, whoever she was, wherever she was, had eaten for lunch — probably fish and rice, neither of which he liked.

At the kitchen sink he washed up—splashed water on his face to clear his mind—then sat down with Linda to eat. As she gave the blessing, he looked around. He had lived here in this house, with Linda and Harvey Carlson, since the age of two—all his life, essentially. He had no memories of his birth mother, but lately his whole life (except at the races) felt odd. Felt strange. After he found and took back his birth name, some doorway, some window had opened inside his head. A dam had broken. Strange thoughts flowed through his brain.

"What time do you have to be at the track?" his mother asked brightly, sitting with him at the table.

He checked his watch. It was 1:45. "In a couple of hours. About four o'clock. Jackster is coming by at three with his pickup and trailer."

"We'll try to get there, though your father has a church board meeting. Hopefully it won't go late."

"No problem if you can't make it," Beau said. In truth, he preferred to go racing alone. Or, more precisely, with his motley group of high school friends who crewed No. 19z. They kept him laughing, kept him from thinking strange thoughts. Cars in general and racing in particular kept Beau's brain from eating itself.

His mother pushed a bowl of lime-green Jell-O his way. "We'll try to be there. Though I have something to confess."

"What's that?" Beau said, suspending a large spoonful of macaroni in midair.

"Sometimes at the races when you're driving?"

"Yeah?"

"I close my eyes and just listen to the announcer," his mother said. "I can't bear to watch."

Beau smiled and touched his mother's arm. "Really, Mom, top speed is about sixty-five miles per hour, plus I wear a helmet, a racing suit, and I'm strapped into a shoulder harness. Statistically, racing is safer than driving down the highway."

"Still," his mother said dubiously. She took small helpings of macaroni and Jell-O.

"Didn't you eat already?" Beau asked.

"No. I thought I'd wait for you."

Beau smiled. "Thanks. Hey, if you come tonight, I'll burn a donut just for you. It'll be my signal that everything's okay."

She managed a smile and passed him the white bread. "Actually, it might rain tonight," she said. "Over fifty percent chance, the weather girl says."

"It can't rain," Beau said. "Not on race night."

"The rain is in God's hands, not ours," his mother said.

Beau kept eating.

"By the way, Amber called."

Beau looked sideways at his mother.

"I told her you were working on the car and couldn't be disturbed."

"Thanks," Beau said, and returned to eating.

His mother paused. "How come you won't take her calls?"

"Because she annoys me."

"It's that sponsor thing, isn't it?"

"No!" Beau said too loudly, too quickly.

"Well," his mother said, "it's not like she's a bad driver."

"You think if she were a guy she'd have a local sponsor?" Beau shot back. "I seriously doubt it."

His mother shrugged. "All I know is, whenever I've been to the races, she always finishes well up on the pack, plus the fans like her. It's fun to root for a girl once in a while—and she's cute. All that red hair."

"Cute," Beau said with a snort. "That's what Amber's all about: cute. If I had a sponsor, I'd whip her butt every Saturday night."

"Don't be unkind," his mother said. "And anyway, she said to wish you good luck."

Beau eyeballed his mother. "Really? She said that?"

His mother nodded, but her blue eyes twinkled.

"What else did she say?" Beau pressed.

"Actually, she said, 'Tell Beau good luck—he's going to need it.' "

AMBER

"Paper or plastic?"

In the grocery checkout line with her two whining children rocking the cart, an overweight mother gave Am-

ber a blank look. Amber Jenkins, eighteen, a stubby straw-
berry blonde with green eyes and freckles, waited. Seconds ticked away. At least five seconds of her life—totally
lost. All she wanted to do was finish her shift at three
(only eighty-two minutes left), get home, and spend time
with her car. Get her racing head on.

"It's not that difficult a question," Amber said.

The till guy, Darin, went round-eyed—then threw a
hand to his mouth to cover a laugh.

The mother blinked. "What did you say?" she asked
Amber.

"Ah, paper or plastic?"

"No, after that."

"Nothing, really," Amber said, her cheeks starting to
warm. "At least I don't think so."

"Yes, you did. Didn't she?" The woman turned to
Darin as her kids began to rattle the cart louder and shout
for candy.

"Excuse me?" Darin asked, as if hadn't heard her question, let alone what Amber said.

The woman gave him a dark look. "I want to see the
manager."

"Todd to lane 4, Todd to lane 4!" Darin said immediately into his microphone. Amber shot him a glare as he
continued to swipe the lady's groceries.

"Watch my kids," the woman said to Darin as she
stepped away to speak with Todd.

"Now I'm the babysitter, thanks!" Darin hissed to Amber. He looked cross-eyed at the kids, who drew back and shut up.

Amber tugged plastic bags quietly from a sheaf of them (when in doubt, go plastic). Soon Todd, the assistant manager dweeb, arrived. As the woman spoke to him, he kept nodding and staring at Amber. Then he came her way.

"Now you've finally done it," Darin whispered. The other checkout clerks, watching, waiting for the fun part, moved their arms at half speed; the beeping of their scanners slowed as if the store were some giant toy and its battery was going dead.

"Amber?" Todd said sternly.

"Yes?"

"I want you to apologize to this woman."

"Apologize?"

"For being rude."

"Ah, sorry," Amber muttered.

"Sorry for what?" Todd asked.

"Sorry . . . that I was rude and crabby. Paper or plastic —who cares, really?" She flashed a fake smile.

"We care," Todd replied. "We care about everything— especially our customers here at EconoMart. Amber, I want you to finish bagging her groceries and get her and her fine children on their way. We've wasted enough of her time."

"Sure. No problem," Amber said; she kept her eyes down as she finished bagging.

"We've had trouble with her before," Todd said to the

woman. He shot a glance at Amber. "An *attitude* thing. And, Amber? When you get back, please meet me in my office."

Darin smirked.

Out in the parking lot, Amber pushed the woman's cart dutifully down Cardinal Row. The kids were screaming for real now, and Amber played her usual guess-the-car game. The best thing about being a carryout girl was that she got to be outside at least half the time—that and check out people's cars. You could tell almost everything about a person by his or her car. Ninety percent of the time she could guess the car a person drove. She angled toward the dented Dodge Grand Caravan, 1996 or '97, with glass heavily smudged on the inside.

"In the side," the woman said. Most of the time, people didn't realize that she had guessed their cars; it was like they expected carryout kids to be mind readers.

"No problem," Amber said cheerfully.

As the woman strapped in her kids from the other side door, Amber stowed the bags, one by one, so they wouldn't tip over. As she bent low to lift a twenty-four-pack of Mountain Dew, her gaze went to the asphalt. From beneath the van snaked a pencil-wide stream of antifreeze. She dipped her head to peek under the van. A fluorescent-green drop splashed down, and then another.

"Ah, ma'am?" Amber said, straightening up and stowing the Dew.

"What?" the woman said as she cinched in the last kid.

"Your van has a leak."

The woman stared. The blank look again. For some reason Amber glanced at her left hand: no wedding ring, which likely meant she was either a single mom or divorced.

"A leak? Where?"

Amber pointed to the asphalt, then knelt to point underneath. The woman bent down to look. "You're losing engine coolant," Amber said.

"Is it bad?" the woman asked.

"Well, it could be," Amber said. "Has your engine been overheating?"

The woman's blank look returned. "I don't know."

"Your dashboard gauge would tell you. The gauge or the idiot light."

The woman glared.

"I mean—that's what everybody calls them, 'idiot lights,' " Amber said quickly. "Gauges are way better, because you can watch them for any changes. Idiot lights only come on when there's something wrong—and then sometimes it's too late."

The woman shrugged. "I don't know what I have." Her voice faltered slightly at the end, as if this was the last straw in a very bad day. As if she was going to come undone in a major way.

"I could take a look," Amber said, with a quick glance over her shoulder toward the store. "Go ahead and start the engine."

"So how do you know about cars?" the woman asked as she turned the key.

"I sort of come from a car family," Amber said, and left it at that.

The woman shrugged. "My husband used to do all the car stuff. But he's in Montana now. I think." Her kids poked at one another and tried to wrestle out of their car seats.

Amber thrust her head inside over the steering wheel. "No gauges. Have you noticed any warning lights?"

"I don't know," the woman said. "You kids behave back there!"

"Go ahead and let it idle, and we'll wait to see if a light comes on," Amber said. She glanced again over her shoulder at the store. No Todd lurking in the window, spying on her—often he timed the carryout kids, recording how long it took them coming and going. No Todd in the window meant he was probably in his office holding her time card. Waiting.

She turned back to the dashboard. After less than a minute, a yellow light blinked on.

"I'd say you're low on antifreeze," Amber said.

"How do you know it's antifreeze?" the woman asked, suspicious again.

"By color," Amber said. "Antifreeze is nearly always bright green." She pointed sideways to the empty parking slot next to them. "Different fluids have different colors. See those red-colored drips? That's transmission fluid. And that little rainbow splash to the left is gasoline. Those bigger dark patches in the middle of every parking slot—those are engine oil. Every car has a drip of some kind."

"Can I make it home?" the woman asked.

"How far do you have to drive?"

"About a half hour."

Amber frowned. "I don't think you should try," she said. She knelt down to peek underneath. Another big drip splattered down.

"So what do I do? I can't afford a big repair bill." The woman's eyes welled up.

"A coolant leak is not necessarily a big deal," Amber said quickly, standing again. "It could be a hole in your radiator, which can be spendy, but usually it's just a hose that needs replacing or a hose clamp that needs tightening. What you want to do is stop over at Joe's Westside Service on Eighteenth Street. Ask for Joe—he's my brother—and say that Amber sent you. Tell him to check your hoses and clamps."

The woman turned to her kids. "Once and for all, shut up back there!" she ordered. And she drove off with a lurch.

"You're welcome!" Amber said, and shrugged.

She took her time heading back inside—it was probably her last trip anyway. Her eyes scanned the cars and the asphalt as her cart rattled along. It was amazing how many cars had leaks or bad tires. People did not pay attention to their cars. At least a third of all tires in the parking lot were out of alignment—one side worn, the other still good—or else they were underinflated. She had read somewhere that the average driver could save three hundred dollars a year on gasoline if his car's tires were properly inflated. In a recently vacated parking slot was a puddle of fuel big enough to flash and burn if somebody dropped a cigarette. What were people thinking? In the old days, before cars, people had to feed and water their horses and take care of the horses' shoes. Why should it be any different with cars? Back in the day, there must have been a lot of mistreated horses.

Soon she was approaching the wide, bright electric-eye doors—and was surprised to see the woman's Dodge van parked in the yellow-painted pedestrian walk. Annoyed customers flowed around both sides of it. Suddenly the crabby mother came back through the sliding doors (Amber crouched slightly lower behind her cart), got in her van, and lurched off. Amber glanced down at the little puddle of green, then went inside. Darin was grinning. Todd waited for her, color in his neck.

"So am I fired?" Amber asked. She wanted to beat him to the punch.

"No," Todd said. He turned sideways so the others couldn't hear.

"No?" Amber said.

"No. Now get back to work and don't cause any more trouble," he mumbled.

As Todd oozed away to his office, Amber turned to Darin.

"It was hilarious," Darin whispered immediately. "The woman told Todd it was her mistake—that you had not been rude at all. In fact, not only were you *not* rude, you were very helpful—more helpful than any other carryout kid ever. Plus, you'd better not be fired or she would file a complaint against Todd and the store, too."

Amber headed back to her checkout lane—then, on second thought, she headed to Todd's little office.

She tapped on his door.

"What?" he said, pretending to be too busy to look at her.

"Would you mind if I punched out early?" she asked. "I have to go home and check on my car."

SONNY

Senator (Sonny) Down Wind rummaged halfheartedly through a pile of bald tires. Behind him the Pure Stock 1984 Chevy Monte Carlo, red and black No. 66, sat perched on the trailer—which was going nowhere because it had two flat tires.

"I know there's some decent ones in here," Leonard said from the other side of the pile. Leonard was his nephew, who hung around and helped crew on race day.

"If we can't find them, we'll take a couple of tires off your dad's car," Sonny said.

"I don't think so," Leonard said.

Sonny kept turning over the tires, most of them half full of water, some with moss inside. "We should burn this pile. Think of how many mosquitoes we'd kill."

"Mosquitoes don't bother me," Leonard said. "They bother some people, but not me." Over a bald Goodyear he gave Sonny a sly look. It was his dig at Sonny, his own uncle, for being lighter-skinned than himself; it had been their running joke since Leonard was small.

"Yeah, yeah," Sonny said, tumbling a truck tire down at Leonard. "And some people get off the rez once in a while."

"I get off the rez!" Leonard said, standing up. His long dark hair gleamed in the sun. He was a handsome kid, tall, with a straight nose and strong cheekbones, light on his feet, silky smooth with a basketball.

"Yeah, for away ball games maybe."

"More than that," Leonard said.

"Hey, you're seventeen and you don't even have your driver's license," Sonny said.

"What's the big hurry?" Leonard said. "I get around well enough."

"You gotta broaden your horizons—meet people— learn how to get along out there."

"In the white man's world, you mean?"

"It's everybody's world," Sonny said. "If you approach it that way, it becomes that way."

"I like it here," Leonard said. "On the rez everybody knows me."

"Nobody really knows you," Sonny said. Leonard grinned at that. He truly was too shy, a boy who opened up only around Sonny.

"Keep looking," Leonard said, kicking aside some more baldies. "You won't be going anywhere tonight unless we find two more decent tires."

Sonny sat down on the pile, then leaned back and stared up at the sky. An eagle, very high up, barely a brown speck, rode the updrafts. He was probably watching them right now. Eagles had eyes like telescopes; they could see everything. "I think the Tall Chiefs are gone to Minneapolis this weekend," Sonny said suddenly. "We could borrow the tires off that Pontiac, then get them back on before they get home."

Leonard dropped the tire he was inspecting. "They'd be pissed if they found out."

"How they gonna find out?"

Leonard scratched his head. "I dunno."

"Neither of us is going to tell them."

"You sure they're gone to the cities?" Leonard asked.

"Positive. They're at a powwow down at Little Earth in Minneapolis."

Leonard reluctantly followed Sonny to Sonny's pickup, a rusty Ford with a tall hunting rack in back.

"Just when I think you're a lost cause, you come back big," Sonny said, slamming the door, firing the engine.

"Yeah, well, remember that this was your idea," Leonard said.

"Hey, even if we get caught, you're home free. You know why?"

Leonard looked at Sonny.

"Because you're riding with a senator. Senators get away with everything." Sonny laughed at his own joke.

Leonard rolled his eyes but cracked a trace of smile.

"You know why my mother—your very own auntie—named me Senator?"

"I know, I know," Leonard said with exaggerated boredom, and looked out his window.

"She named me that because there ain't no real senator ever gonna come from this reservation."

"It's not like I haven't heard that story before," Leonard said.

Sonny laughed again and sped the truck fast down the dusty road. "Really," he said, looking over at Leonard as they flew along. "I think you're just shy. That's why you don't like to go to town."

"Watch the road!" Leonard said.

"All those nice young girls out there," Sonny said, "like that Gurneau girl, Ritchie's daughter—what's her name? Wednesday?"

"Tuesday," Leonard said quickly, "Tudy"—then wished he hadn't.

"Very good," Sonny said. "I hear Tudy's dying to meet you."

"Maybe I don't like girls," Leonard replied.

The truck swerved—Leonard had to grab the wheel to keep them from going into the ditch. When he caught a glimpse of Sonny's face, he laughed like crazy.

"Very funny," Sonny said, batting Leonard's hands from the wheel.

Leonard leaned back, pleased with himself.

They drove along another quarter mile, then Sonny gave him serious look. "Funny, right? You're joking, yes?"

Leonard said, "Watch the road, Mr. Senator—you'll kill us both."

TUDY

Tuesday Thompson-Gurneau (everybody called her Tudy) smelled like pork. She was fifteen, and all summer long she smelled like pork. Pulled pork, jerked pork, barbecued pork, smoked pork, racks of pork ribs. Her stepfather, Ritchie Thompson, was the owner of Ritchie's BBQ Waggin, and she had to work for him. For him and her mother, Winona, who also helped out summers. Her parents towed the silvery metal trailer with its slide-out cookers and propane burners to races, weddings, class reunions, powwows—even a funeral now and then. Her mom's corner of the trailer had a deep-fat cooker, where she made fry bread from a recipe she had brought down from her people on their Canadian reserve. The Thompson-Gurneau family made good money during the summer (her mother was an elementary school teacher the rest of the year), but for her stepfather, barbecue was twelve months and then some.

All Ritchie thought about, all he talked about, all he read about was barbecue. Most dads read hunting and fishing or else sports and auto racing magazines. Her father read everything there was on barbecue, including books from experts in all the different "schools": Kansas-style barbecue, New Orleans–style barbecue, and so on.

Right now he was semidozing in his lawn chair beside the trailer and its wisps of stinky pork smoke. A couple of neighborhood dogs lurked in the bushes; they knew they'd get some leftovers later that night, when the races were over, but they'd come early just in case. They smelled the wagon. Or maybe they smelled her.

Once at a powwow, she took a break to watch the dancers. As she walked along the grounds, some Leech Lake girls began to laugh and point at her. Turning, Tudy saw the dogs—a half dozen scruffy dogs—trailing close behind, sniffing at her jeans. It was the most embarrassing moment of her life. Now, she grabbed a pebble and pitched it hard at the two neighborhood dogs; they jumped away, then sulked just out of range.

If smelling like pork was one embarrassment, the other big one was having a white man for a stepfather. Ritchie Thompson was a pudgy guy in a spotted butcher's apron; his jaw was slacked open and his eyes closed to slits. He had been up all night pulling the pork, simmering the secret sauce. Now, while the ribs slow-cooked, he rested—but downwind of the smoke. In case something went wrong—a pan overheated—he could smell it and spring into action and save the ribs.

"Hey, Tudy," Ritchie said to her.

She said nothing.

"Everything okay?"

She shrugged, then looked for a rock to throw at the dogs.

"Your mother got her dough ready?"

"Yes," Tudy said crabbily.

"You and her going to town soon to get the buns, right?"

"Yes!" Tudy said. The dogs crept closer. She slowly leaned her right arm down to get a bigger pebble this time.

Ritchie scratched his belly. "I was thinking. Maybe this winter, after Christmas, we should take a family-type vacation. Get away from here, see some country."

Tudy listened as she watched the dogs.

"Drive down to Texas, then across the border into Mexico," he said.

"We could go to Cancún!" Tudy said. "For spring break. Where all the college kids go!"

"I'd like to see how the Mexicans do pork down there," Ritchie said, a faraway look in his eyes.

"I quit!" Tudy muttered, pitching her stone at the dogs, then stalking away.

Inside the house, her mother kneaded a fat white mound of bread dough. Her dark hair was pulled back, and she wore round, dangly dream-catcher earrings. "What's the matter, honey?"

"Why didn't you stay married to Dad? Tell me one more time."

"He had girlfriends from one end of the reserve to the other. Simple as that."

Tudy was silent. "And why did you marry Ritchie?"

Her mother smiled and did not break her rhythm. She looked out the window. "Ritchie might look like the laziest guy in the world," she said. "But you and I know he's been up all night. He works hard. He doesn't have time to fool around like your dad."

"But pork," Tudy said with a groan. "A barbecue wagon. Why not, say, an accountant. Or a lawyer?"

"The summer's zipping right along, dear," Winona said patiently. "We're already at the halfway point."

"I *hate* working the wagon!" Tudy said. "People who know me—kids from school—they see me all greasy and sweaty. It's a totally humiliating summer job."

"No, it's your college money, remember?" her mother said, her wrists and long fingers turning the dough with an easy, rolling motion.

"I'm not going to college!" Tudy said, and stamped off to her room.

"You're going to college," her mother said quickly after her. Then her tone lightened. "After all, where else could you meet an accountant or a lawyer?"

"Aaaargh!" Tudy shouted, and slammed her door.

THE WEATHER

It has no true name. People say, "It's going to rain." Or "It's hot today." But what do they mean by "it"? No one ever says.

The weather has no real name, just as it has no real home. It blows where it blows, it stops when it stops. It takes its orders from the sun and season, from the tilt of the earth. It couldn't care less about what goes on at ground level—at ball games, picnics, and speedways.

On this Saturday, a mass of cold air pushed slowly into western North Dakota. Blown from Siberia across the Bering Strait, rotating counterclockwise through Alaska, then southeast into Canada, the low-pressure system showed up as a long green blotch on weather radar screens.

In its path was a warm front, a belly of humid gulf air over five hundred miles long. Stalled along the North Dakota–Minnesota border, the front had gathered itself over two weeks of travel up from the Gulf of Mexico. It was packing heavy humidity—hundreds of tons of mois-

ture. The warm front was overextended. It needed to rest
and gather its powers, but the low-pressure system was approaching, its chilly breath testing the underside of the
warm front's western edge. As the cooler air advanced, a
roll cloud wound itself into a horizontal blue-gray tube between the fronts. At ground level, deer and birds lifted
their heads to sniff the air. Stirring, they began to feed toward cover, toward their beds and nests. They could smell
rain.

Saturday

3:00 P.M.

TRACE

"Bump it again," Larry said. He was bent over the engine compartment of the Bonham Street Stock—which was still in the shop.

From his aluminum racing seat, Trace blipped the ignition switch. The cylinder heads, valve train, and valve covers were finally in place, but he was not ready to start the motor. He was cranking over the engine to find top dead center, or TDC, valve position. From there Larry could set the distributor in place—all in preparation for engine timing. Trace glanced at his watch. Other teams and their cars were already at the track. They were checking in, unloading, setting up. A headache began to throb just behind Trace's eyes. The unobstructed view of Larry's hairy lower back and butt crack didn't help.

"Again," Larry called, squinting with concentration.

Trace tweaked the ignition switch. The spark plug for

cylinder number 1 lay on the fender; Larry had his thumb over its empty little porthole to the cylinder and was waiting to feel the exhaust stroke—a puff of compressed air.

"Got it!" Larry said.

Trace remained in the car as Larry fit the distributor pole in place, then added the rotor and distributor cap. Last he attached the eight spark plug wires to the top of the distributor.

"Get 'em right," Trace murmured.

The bottom, starting line of engine performance was the cylinders—eight of them—firing in the right sequence. For Chevrolet engines, the order of firing was 1, 8, 4, 3, 6, 5, 7, 2. This sequence was stamped on the engine block in case the mechanic forgot it, but a true motor head such as Trace had the numbers stamped on his brain.

Once, in ninth-grade history class during a unit on World War II, Mr. Jorgenson, the teacher, was talking about famous spies when Trace suddenly raised his hand. Melody Walters sat two rows over, and he was probably trying to show off, but he also had an idea. "Yes, Trace?" Mr. Jorgenson asked; he was clearly surprised that Trace was volunteering something. "I just thought of the perfect interrogation question to screen out foreign spies and terrorists," Trace said. Mr. Jorgenson paused. "Better than who won the last World Series, that kind of question?" "Way better," Trace said confidently. "Okay, let's hear it," the teacher said. "What is 18436572?" Trace replied. Several motor heads in class perked up for the first time all term. Mr. Jorgenson got a blank look, then said, "Explain." Trace laid out the meaning of 18436572 as it related to Chevy engines. "I mean, what better way to tell if somebody is really an American?" he finished. Mr. Jorgenson stared long moments at Trace, then said, "Could we try to stay focused here?" There was laughter in the room, Melody seemed embarrassed, and Trace never raised his hand in that class again.

"All right, fire it up," Larry said.

Trace cranked over the engine for real this time. The 350-cubic-inch Chevy caught on the second revolution and snarled to life—then settled into a steady rumble at 1200 rpm. But "rumble" was not what they were looking for; "rumble" was an engine out of tune. Trace felt the shudder and shake in the seat of his jeans and in his spine.

"It's not running right," he called out the window.

"Like I can't tell?" Larry said.

Trace bit his lip.

Larry leaned back and scratched his chin. "So what do you think is the problem, Mr. Mechanic?"

"Plug wires on right?"

"Yes," Larry said with annoyance.

Trace blipped the accelerator, then listened. "There's no lag when I punch it," he called over the noise. "The engine doesn't fall on its face, so it's not carburetor- or fuel system–related."

"So what, then?"

Trace realized Larry was fishing; he didn't have a clue. "It's got to be the timing," Trace said.

"Maybe," Larry allowed.

Trace let the engine idle and pulled himself backward through the window opening.

"Not enough advance—that's probably our trouble," Larry said, reaching for the timing light. He was the kind of mechanic who came up with a theory, then tried to make the facts fit.

Trace watched as Larry clumsily hooked the alligator clip of the black ground wire to the engine frame.

"Want me to do it?" Trace asked. "I don't mind," he added quickly.

Larry paused, then shrugged. "Suit yourself. I'll turn the distributor cap until it runs right."

Trace double-checked the ground wire, then clipped the red wire onto the number 1 spark plug wire. With the engine running at idle speed, he bent forward and pointed the handheld "pistol" light at the front base of the engine—to its crankshaft pulley and its spinning hash marks. He watched the tiny marks on the pulley flicker in the white strobe light that flashed in time with the spark plug. The final goal of engine timing was to make sure the intake (air and gasoline) valves and exhaust valves on each cylinder opened and closed at the right moment. There was engine timing for standard highway driving, but the timing could be altered—advanced—to increase horsepower.

"We're at twenty-eight now," Trace said. "Keep going."

Beside him, Larry slowly rotated the distributor cap. He was sweating now, and smelled like French fries. The engine shuddered worse than before.

"Let's go to thirty-four degrees," Larry said, and turned the distributor accordingly.

"Still no good," Trace said above the ragged, throaty rhythm. He straightened up and looked at the distributor. "Maybe we dropped the distributor pole in wrong. It could be a cog off TDC."

"No way," Larry growled. "I did it myself. It's not the distributor." Sweat leaked from his sideburns. He wiped his face with a grease rag and glanced at his watch.

Trace's watch read 3:19 p.m. His headache throbbed worse than the out-of-tune engine.

"Once we get out to the track and run a few laps, we'll get it figured out," Larry said, clamping the distributor back in place.

"I thought the goal was to get the car ready before we arrive," Trace said—this time plenty loud enough for Larry to hear.

"You worry too much, kid," Larry said, and began to toss tools into open drawers.

"Do you mind if I at least look at some things?"

"Suit yourself. Just don't break anything."

Trace leaned on the fender and examined the distributor, rotor, and cap—all fine. He turned to the Holley carburetor. Its two venturi "horns," or intakes, looked fine

—no constriction or obstructions. The throttle linkage and springs were all in order. As Trace worked, Larry lingered in the shop. Trace got the feeling that the older man was watching him; whenever he glanced over, Larry quickly looked away. Then it hit Trace—a thought that rocked his brain like a motor throwing a rod. Larry didn't want yellow No. 32 to run right.

MEL

"Mel—we've got trouble with the grader," George said.

"Hang on, George," Mel said into her headset, then turned back to her cell phone. "Yes, there's racing tonight, hot laps at six, heats at seven, features starting at eight." Didn't people read the newspaper? Then there was Trace himself, who had called "just wanting to talk." She was way too busy for that. Right now her focus was on hunting down race teams sitting in the rain. That meant western Minnesota, along with the Fargo and Grand Forks areas. To avoid competition, tracks within an hour or so from each other held races on different nights. It was rained-out Saturday night tracks that she focused on.

"The grader, George? Say again?" she said into her mouthpiece.

"Can't get it started."

Mel's shoulders sagged, and she let out a short breath.

"We could pull it, get the motor turning over, and then jump-start it," George added. "But I need somebody to drive the tow truck for me."

Mel looked around for her father. He was on his four-wheeler over in the pit area welcoming drivers (so far all local), checking them in, getting their signatures on liability release forms. Her gaze went to Maurice, arriving in his bright whites and carrying his tidy case of flags.

"No way," George said. "We wouldn't want to get Maurice's pants dirty."

George and Maurice did not get along.

"I could help you myself," Mel began, but the phone rang again.

"How about the parking lot kid?" George asked, jerking his head to Patrick, who was over by the chain-link fence yanking again and again on the cord of a weed-cutting string trimmer.

"Probably not," Mel said quickly.

"He's got a driver's license, doesn't he?" George asked.

"Okay—give him a try," Mel said, lifting the phone to her ear.

As George turned away, she held the phone briefly to her T-shirt and called after him. "Make sure he doesn't run over you!"

George gave her a thumbs-up signal and headed off.

Mel's call—a callback—was from Viking Speedway in Alexandria. A woman in the announcer's booth gave her a phone number for one of the Late Model teams.

"Thanks!" Mel said. She dialed the number.

"Yeah?" a man said on the first ring. He sounded annoyed—like he was having a very bad day.

"This is Mel Walters up at Headwaters Speedway—"

"Mel? Headwaters? You're breaking up. My phone doesn't work worth a damn when there's weather around," the man said.

"Is it raining there?" Mel asked quickly.

"It's gonna. Dark skies and lightning just to the west." Static crackled in the phone like shaken aluminum foil.

"Hello?"

"Still here," the man said.

Mel spoke rapidly. "I'm calling to spread the word. Here at Headwaters we've got clear skies, not a cloud in sight." Well, a few clouds. "We've got a full lineup of racing tonight."

"Is that so?" the man said, his voice sounding louder. In the background, thunder rumbled. "This is Cal Hopkins, by the way."

It was Mel's turn to go silent. "Cal Hopkins—as in green No. 42?"

"That'd be me," he said. "A bunch of us Late Model guys are stuck here in Alex. We were supposed to race tonight. We need a tune-up for Cedar Lake next weekend, but things don't look good."

"Why not drive up here?" Mel said. "It's only a couple hours or so."

There was brief dead airspace.

"Hello?"

"Keep talking," Cal said.

"We're racing tonight," Mel said quickly. "That's a guarantee."

"A guarantee," Cal Hopkins said with a laugh. He had a sexy voice; Mel felt herself blush. "I like your confidence, young lady," he said. "Who is this, again?"

"Mel—Melody—Walters. I'm the track manager. Johnny Walters's daughter?"

There was a long moment of silence. "Johnny Walters's daughter?"

"That's right."

There was another pause, as if Cal Hopkins had something more to say, but he didn't. "I don't know," he said. "It's pretty short notice."

"I can push back hot laps—the feature, too—if that would help."

There was another pause. "Tell you what, Melody. I'll talk to my crew. My guess is, they'll probably want to come, but—"

"Great! And if you know of any other drivers sitting in the rain, maybe you could let them know we're good to go?"

"I suppose I could do that," Cal said. "If it rains here, Golden Spike down in St. Cloud will probably get rained out, too."

"Oh—and one more thing!" Mel said.

"Yes?" Cal said, a trace of annoyance in his voice.

"If—when—you come through town, could you make a loop down Main Street? If the locals saw your cars, it would boost the gate here at the speedway."

"Why aren't you working for me instead of Johnny?" Cal said. "I'll check with my crew and see what they think."

After Cal Hopkins rang off, Mel pumped a fist in the air and let out a whoop.

MAURICE

In his small square fo'c's'le (pronounced "forecastle" only by landlubbers), the old sailor arranged his colored flags. Like a ship captain's deck, Maurice's flag stand stood dead center, at the lower edge of the grandstand. Perched about ten feet above the dirt, it had the commanding view of the track. Cars ran just below the tidy white-painted deck with white wooden railing.

As Maurice placed flags in their slots, across the track in the pit area tools clattered and banged. Steel ramps thudded onto the ground as crews rolled race cars from covered car-hauler trailers. Generators fired up and hummed. Pneumatic impact wrenches rattled like machine guns firing as they ratcheted lug nuts against steel rims. Drivers, testing their cars, spun the tires and raced the engines. The sounds collected against the green wall of aspen trees beyond the speedway fence, then echoed back across the infield. They were the sounds of the speedway coming alive.

Maurice paused to watch George and Patrick walk across the track. The young man wore clean jeans and nice boots—in contrast to George and his shabby coveralls and ancient hat. George was a disgrace to the speedway. It was a good thing he spent most of his time in the pit area, or else inside the truck. He looked like a hobo.

In Maurice's opinion, the entire speedway needed a makeover. Or at least a top-to-bottom cleaning, including fresh paint and some fresh people to work there. The toilet buildings were shabby. The concession area was a disgrace—it was a wonder the state health department hadn't shut it down. The pit area had old wreckers and tow trucks and half-tractors. Behind them were faded signs from sponsors who had gone out of business twenty years ago. Weeds and small trees were creeping in. Soon they'd take over.

Maurice brought out his little whisk broom and began to sweep his flagman's platform. When finished, he stood there with both hands on the railing. In his white pants, with his flags ready, he always felt like he was back aboard ship. Back where things were orderly—not like the world today. In the Navy, when ships were under radio silence, the flagman communicated ship to ship with only his semaphore flags and his flag hoists. All the sailors knew what the colors meant. That was what he liked about racing: flags and colors still meant something. There was still some order left, some rules to follow. He checked his watch. Only two hours and six minutes until hot laps.

BEAU

Beau's crew—all three of them—leaned over No. 19z, still parked in his parents' garage. Dweeb, Guitar Hero, and Jackster shouted back and forth above loud music and engine noise as they sucked on Jolt and Mountain Dew. Having a race car, even a beater like Beau's, was a fairly cool thing in high school, so it was not difficult to find a crew. Well, it was a little more difficult because of the four-cylinder thing, but there were just enough import nuts in high school who drove older, tricked-out Honda Civics and boosted Toyota Corollas to form an actual club (Beau was president). The club, named Imports Rule, irritated farmers such as Trace Bonham and his V-8 crowd to no end—which was why Beau's club chose that name. It was a mostly friendly rivalry, one that kept Beau and his friends occupied by thinking up clever ways to annoy the big-block V-8 boys.

"That stuff will ruin your teeth," Beau called. "A couple more years of Mountain Dew and you'll have meth mouth."

"I'll sacrifice teeth for caffeine any day," Dweeb shouted. He had a mass of naturally blond dreadlocks, which was why they called him Dweeb. Dreadlocks, everyone agreed (except for Dweeb), just did not make it on Caucasian guys.

Guitar Hero, a tall, skinny ninth-grader, was a slashing, for-real guitarist—and not bad with tools. He was checking the six bolts, nuts, and washers on Beau's racing seat. A true tech head, he was also great with electrical and wiring issues.

Jackster, the only one besides Beau who really knew four-cylinder engines, was blipping the throttle and listening. "If we bored it sixty-thousandths over, you'd beat Amber every time."

"Amber? Do I know an Amber?" Beau said.

Dweeb yukked it up. Guitar Hero grinned.

"Sorry," Jackster said to Beau. "I still think we should bore this block sixty-thousandths over, and get a performance cam, too. Then you could compete with Amber."

"And who would pay for the boring and the cam?" Beau asked.

Jackster looked up suddenly. "Hey—we could hold a raffle."

"Yeah!" Dweeb said with enthusiasm.

"Or better yet, a benefit!" Jackster added. "Like those sad posters you always see in cafés and gas stations? 'Benefit for Billy Butthead for medical expenses after The Accident.' They never say what The Accident was. But ours would be a benefit for No. 19z Engine Boring, Honing, and Cam."

"Yeah," said Guitar Hero with excitement (he was the

most gullible of the three). "I'll bet your mom would cook."

Dweeb and Jackster collapsed with laughter. "As if anyone would come," Dweeb said.

Guitar Hero turned his attention to the roof frame. He tugged on the horizontal steel support over the driver's door. "Whoa!" he said.

"What?" Beau asked.

"Look at this," Guitar Hero said, leaning close. "There's a crack in the weld."

"Yeah, I know," Beau said. "I told you I got the chassis from a wreck."

"Still," Guitar Hero said dubiously. Dweeb turned off the engine; he and Jackster came over to look closely at the two-inch-by-two-inch square-channel lengths of steel.

"The weld's broken almost all the way through," Dweeb said.

"Don't pull on it!" Beau said. "You want to wreck my car?"

None of his crew laughed. The music paused between tracks.

"Are you sure you should be driving this?" Guitar Hero asked. "The roll cage is a little sketchy, too, if you ask me."

"It's a perfectly good roll cage," Beau said, reaching inside and pulling on the round pipe. The car rocked back and forth. "See?" He had fixed the roll cage himself. First he filled the inch-and-a-half-diameter, thirteen-gauge replacement pipe sections with sand. Then he applied heat from a propane torch. Next he bent the pipes around a tree trunk (the sand prevented the pipe from crimping) to the correct curves and angles. Last came the welding. "It's plenty strong."

At that moment, Beau's mom popped her head through the door. "Hi, boys. I baked some cookies."

They stared at her.

She stared back. "Is everything all right?"

"Sure," Beau said quickly.

"You all had these guilty looks on your faces—like when you were little and had broken a window or something." She smiled.

Beau manufactured a laugh. "Just working, Mom, that's all. We'll be there in a second."

After Linda left, the four of them looked at one another.

"I still say—" Guitar Hero began, but Beau cut him off.

"Okay, okay, I'll weld it again—don't worry about it!"

"Yeah! On to the cookies, dudes," Dweeb said, and bolted toward the kitchen door.

PATRICK

"You want me to drive the wrecker?"

"That's right," George said. "Is that a problem?"

"Ah, no," Patrick said quickly.

George's eyes went to the string trimmer. "Problems with that thing?"

Patrick shrugged. "Won't start."

George took it, put his nose close to the spark plug. "Flooded, but not bad." He clicked the switch back and forth, then yanked the string. The trimmer coughed, burned off its excess gas-oil mix, then settled into a steady hum.

"What'd you do?" Patrick asked.

"You had the on-off switch in the wrong position." Patrick's shoulders slumped.

"Easy to do," George said. "The new equipment is all made in China or someplace—the switches never say 'on' or 'off' anymore. Just those little zeros and slash marks. I've got a new chain saw like that. Drives me crazy."

Patrick was surprised at how helpful George was. He'd barely said hello on previous Saturdays.

"Anyway, come with me, kid. I need you to help me start the grader."

Patrick's shoulders straightened. Walking with George through the gate and onto the track—a place he'd never been before—shot goose bumps across his arms. The dirt was lumpier and rougher than he'd imagined; from a distance it looked way smoother. He followed George carefully so as not to scuff his boots. He tried to imagine what it was like to drive a race car. Crossing the track, he glanced around to see if Mel was watching. She wasn't.

"We're all hooked on," George said as they approached the grader.

Patrick slowed his walk. Up close, the old yellow open-seated Galion grader was huge—the wheels were as high as his shoulders; its iron blade, hung with clumps of mud, looked impossibly heavy.

"The wrecker's old, but it runs fine," George said, holding open the door. "Start out in first gear, real slow. Give it lots of gas. The grader's heavy."

Patrick stared into the cab. It was filled with used coffee cups, cookie wrappers, cigar butts, a couple of wool shirts, various tools, such as heavy hammers and pry bars. The seat was ripped. Gray duct tape held down the coil springs. The interior smelled like a cross between a dog kennel and a garbage can. There was barely room to sit.

"It needs cleaning," George said.

"It's not that."

"Well, what?"

"I've never really driven a stick shift. My older sister has a Toyota with a manual. She taught me, but she doesn't let me drive it."

George reached behind his head to scratch the base of his skull; his cap bill tilted an inch lower on his forehead. "Well, there's no time to learn like the present," he said.

Patrick stared at the cable and hook attached to the grader.

"Tell you what, we'll unhook the cable and you can make a couple of test starts. Now hop to it," George said.

Patrick swallowed and climbed inside the wrecker as George clattered around with the cable. Patrick gripped the gearshift with his right hand, tested the clutch with his foot. It had a surprisingly strong spring.

"All clear," George said. "Put her in neutral and start it up." He stood on the running board to instruct.

Patrick fumbled with the clutch and shifter until the tall stick slid loosely side to side.

"Bring up the rpm and keep letting out the pedal," George said. "It doesn't engage until the very—"

Patrick let the clutch out all the way—too quickly at the last—and the wrecker lurched forward. George tried to hang on but tumbled in the dirt—luckily onto a soft spot in the clay—as the wrecker bucked and lurched down the track like a rodeo bull.

"The clutch!" George shouted. "Push in the clutch!"

Patrick jammed in the clutch pedal, and the runaway wrecker coasted to a stop. He let out a breath. "Sorry! You all right?" he called back to George.

"Yes. Fine. Try it again," George said, standing up and brushing mud off his knees.

Patrick set himself, then worked the pedal, the accelerator, and the shift—and made a decent surge forward this time. With a brief grinding of the gears, he got the transmission into reverse, then eased the wrecker back toward the grader and into cable range.

"Good—right there," George called.

Glancing triumphantly across the track, Patrick saw Mel and Maurice watching. Maurice was bent over, holding his gut, soundlessly laughing. Mel held the sides of her face like that famous painting of the guy screaming.

"Ignore the peanut gallery," George said crabbily. "Focus on what you're doing."

"Sorry," Patrick said.

George hooked up the cable, and then they were ready. As Patrick inched the wrecker forward, he felt the cable tighten—felt the great weight of the grader behind. Felt it all the way down his spine and into the soles of his boots on the clutch and gas pedal. It was like nothing he'd ever felt before.

"More gas!" George shouted.

Patrick brought up the rpm; the wrecker groaned and squatted its big rear wheels—and the grader began to move.

"Keep going!" George shouted. From the grader's seat, he worked the throttle, choke, and clutch. The grader's engine turned over with a thudding sound—and then roared to life in a blast of smoke from the clattering lid on its tall exhaust pipe.

With a few jerks, Patrick brought the wrecker to a stop. He hopped out and unhooked the cable. George gave him a big thumbs-up and then a circling motion with his index finger as he pointed to the pit area.

Patrick leaped back into the wrecker and drove around turn 2 toward the pit entrance. Driving alone on the banked track was also like nothing he'd experienced before. He hung his arm out the window. Adjusted the rickety rearview mirror. He shifted into second gear—

which worked just fine. Brought up his speed. Stick shifts were no big deal. He looked across at the stands, where a few early-bird spectators were already putting down their blankets and stadium seats. Mel was heading up the bleachers to the announcer's booth. The sun shone on her tanned long legs, which moved like finely oiled scissors as she took the wooden steps two at a time. Watching her, Patrick missed the pit entrance and had to go around again.

AMBER

When she got home after work and took one look at her car, Amber froze. She stared. Lance knelt beside her little No. 13a, welder's mask down. A river of sparks—like a Fourth of July sparkler—sprayed off his welding rod where it touched the last piece of steel he had hung on the driver's side. Both sides of her boxy red car had steel plating added to the tin skin. Its tires sagged under the new weight.

"What are you *doing*?" Amber shouted—then caught herself.

Lance whirled and held the welding rod like a bayonet.

"It's me, Amber," she said quickly.

He flipped up the mask. She had gotten used to his face, his skull, but there were moments—like this one—

when she forgot. Forgot the flattened left side of his head. Forgot the huge dent there. Forgot the patchwork of stitching that looped down around his droopy left eye. Only a sister, a brother, or parents could ever really get used to how Lance looked—which was why he stayed home most of the time, except for his monthly trips to the Veterans Hospital in Minneapolis.

"Looks like you've been busy!" she said.

He blinked and nodded. "I think this will do it, kid," he said. "Hillbilly armor. You don't want to leave home without it," he said. He laughed, but no sound came out of his saggy mouth.

"The thing of it is, Lance, you *are* home," Amber said. She moved slowly but cautiously toward him; when she was close enough, she leaned over to shut off the humming welder.

For a long moment Lance glanced around the garage. Then he turned to her. "I know that!" he said, suddenly angry.

Amber kept smiling. It was important to speak slowly, move slowly. "I know you know that. I'm just wondering why all the up-armoring on my car."

" 'Cause you're my baby sister, that's why," Lance said—and began to weep.

The swings of emotion, the instant mood changes were Lance's biggest issue. And now they were the whole family's issue. Lance had been in Iraq for two tours, and he came back with part of his skull blown away from a roadside bomb. Iraq was for two tours, but his bent head was for life.

"I have to race tonight, Lance," Amber said. Gently. Softly. "My little old red No. 13a probably weighs a ton—literally."

Lance wiped his eyes and stared at the car. "But it's safe. Nothing's going to happen to you," he said.

"You were going to work on the rear end," Amber said. "Weld gussets on those braces. That was all."

Lance's face scrunched in on itself, and his blue eyes welled over with tears again.

"But, hey, I kinda like the look," she said quickly. "Nobody's going to challenge me in the turns."

Lance snuffled his nose into his hand, wiped it on his dirty jeans.

"I tell you what," Amber said. "I'll go make some lemonade for us. Then when I come back, we can work on the car—together."

Lance only stared at his welding.

"No more of that," Amber said. She took his helmet, and while he stared at the car, she grabbed all the welding rods she could see.

"Okay, Lance?" she added.

He just kept staring at the car. Amber went to the kitchen and let out a long breath. She checked the clock. It would be touch and go getting her car back to weight, but first things first. She dug in the freezer for a can of EconoMart frozen lemonade concentrate.

TUDY

"Hurry up in there. We have to go to town," her mother called through the bathroom door.

"I'm coming, I'm coming," Tudy called back. She plucked two more eyebrow hairs—one on each side of her nose, which itself was way too big, but there was nothing she could do about that—then tilted her face left, then right as she looked into the mirror.

"We're leaving in two minutes."

"I told you, just a second!" Tudy shot back. She hurriedly touched up her mascara and rummaged for her lip liner.

"We're only going to the bakery," Winona said, her voice now close against the wooden door. "This is not *Star Search*."

On the way to town, Tudy kept leaning over to look into the right side-view mirror. She pursed her lips and applied lipgloss. She knew her mother wanted to say something in the worst way, so she beat her to the punch. "Are we going to that stupid day-old bakery place again?"

"Yes," her mother said. "There's nothing wrong with day-old buns, Ritchie says, and I agree. It's the barbecue people taste, not the buns."

"Enough with the barbecue," Tudy said. "I just don't like the people who go there. They look like they're homeless or something."

Winona glanced over. "Some of them probably are homeless."

"Well, we're not," Tudy said, "and we'll never be."

"No one knows that," Winona said, her voice serious. "Anybody's life can turn on a dime."

As her mother pulled into the bakery, Tudy smacked her lips once more in the mirror, then rummaged in her purse for her sunglasses. The bakery was right on the main highway; with luck no one would see her. "Have you seen my sunglasses?" she quickly asked her mother.

"They're on top of the television at home," she answered.

"Great!" Tudy said.

Her mother parked. The bakery was next door to a pharmacy and an auto parts store.

Tudy looked around through the windshield. "Oh, my God!" she shrieked, then ducked low onto the seat.

"What?" her mother said with alarm.

"It's Sonny's truck with his car."

"Where?" asked her mother, looking over her shoulder.

"Parked across the street by the NAPA store. The car's on the trailer, which means they're heading to the races, which means Leonard's with him."

"Well, it could be worse," her mother answered, opening her door. "They could be in the bakery."

"I'm not getting out," Tudy said.

"Yes, you are," her mother said.

Tudy grabbed the stick shift and hung on. "No way!" she said.

Winona stared. "All right. But you have to unload all the buns when we get home."

"Yes, anything!" Tudy hissed, crouching on the floor. "Just go so they don't see you talking to me."

Her mother disappeared for several minutes. Tudy listened to the traffic pass, to people's voices. She prayed that she would hear Sonny's truck start up and leave. Then a grocery cart rattled to a halt, and soft packages of buns began to drop through the window onto the seat. Onto her. Dozens and dozens of buns in bags of twenty-four, falling on her.

"What are you doing!" Tudy whispered as the bun bags fell onto her back and shoulders.

"I thought I'd cover you up," her mother said. "We wouldn't want anyone to see you, right?"

Tudy was about to shout at her mom when Sonny's voice called across the asphalt. "Hey there, Winona—what you doing with all that bad white bread?"

"Hi, Sonny," Winona called back. "Hello, Leonard."

No reply from Leonard.

"Hurry—keep piling them on me!" Tudy whispered.

Her mother did, but she was in no great hurry. Tudy crouched lower and pulled the puffy bags over her as best she could.

"You haven't given up on fry bread, I hope," Sonny said, his teasing voice growing louder.

"No," Winona said, a smile in her voice. "Just stocking up for Ritchie."

"Whew, that's a relief," Sonny said. "Hard to find good Indian fry bread, right, Leonard?"

No reply from Leonard.

"Let me give you a hand with them buns," Sonny said, his boots clacking louder—closer.

"No need," Winona said.

"I don't mind," Sonny said. "Leonard. You grab the rest of those bags."

Tudy scrunched her eyes shut and tried to stay still.

"You want them all in the cab?" Leonard asked softly. His voice had that reservation singsong that Tudy hated.

"Yes—just toss them in there anywhere," Winona said.

Tudy peeked at Leonard's brown arms reaching in and out as he tossed buns on top of her. His brown fingers were long and straight, his nails clean and clipped short. No wonder he could dribble a basketball the way he did— between his legs, then back, between and back, all the while standing there pretending not to notice his admirers, usually some of those little tweeny-bopper girls who hung around the basketball courts.

Daylight shrank, and the bread grew heavier—how could buns weigh so much? Not only that, the yeasty wheat smell made her nose itch. A wall, a dam, of scratchy, itchy air bloomed in her nose, filled her lungs. Her head felt like an overinflated balloon. She clenched her arms over her chest and held her nose as if she were about to go underwater.

"Just enough room," Leonard said, leaning his head through the open window to fit the last bags onto the dashboard—which was when Tudy sneezed.

The bags of buns heaved upward. Leonard let out a shout and jerked back. His head went *clock!* on the top of the truck's window frame. There were startled noises from Sonny and Winona. When Tudy lurched up from beneath the suffocating pile of buns and poked her head out the window, Leonard was lying alongside the truck, knocked out cold.

SONNY

"You're sure you're all right?" Sonny asked Leonard as they drove.

"A few Tweety Birds, but other than that, I'm fine," Leonard said. He rubbed the back of his skull.

Sonny started laughing again.

"It's not all that funny," Leonard said, looking down the road.

"Sorry," Sonny said.

They drove over the Mississippi River inlet bridge, passed the sewage treatment plant, then turned east toward the speedway.

"So she was hiding under the bread?" Sonny asked, biting back a grin.

Leonard shrugged.

"Hiding from you—that's a good sign," Sonny offered.

Leonard glanced sideways at him.

"It means she likes you," Sonny said.

"Right," Leonard said.

"Seriously. Women are strange that way. Whatever they do, you have to figure it means the reverse. There's the story, and then there's the story *behind* the story."

"Huh?" Leonard said.

"Too deep to explain to someone with Tweety Birds on the brain," Sonny said.

"Try me," Leonard said.

Sonny drove on. "I mean, with just about everything in life there's the story, and then there's the *real* story."

"Like?"

"Like, you come along to crew the car, but the main reason you come to the races is to see people. You like to watch them, listen to them, be near them—especially that Tudy girl—because you're basically a shy guy."

Leonard let out an annoyed grunt. "So what's *your* real story?" he shot back.

"Hey, I'm the short-haired Indian guy everybody likes," Sonny said. "King of the reservation Pure Stocks."

"You could get a better ride," Leonard said. "You could move up to Super Stocks or Late Models. Somebody would sponsor you."

"Somebody would own me," Sonny said.

Leonard was silent. After a mile he asked, "Why *don't* you grow your hair out?"

"Then I'd be a different kind of Indian," Sonny said. "I like riding the fence. Best of both worlds. You should try it," he said, tugging at Leonard's ponytail.

"Ouch," Leonard said.

"Sorry—forgot about your Tweety Birds."

They rolled on. After a while, Leonard glanced slyly at Sonny. "Maybe you're scared of Super Stocks and Late Models. Secretly you think they're too much car for you."

"Ouch," Sonny said, and kept driving.

THE WEATHER

The cold front came in low, wedging like a snowplow underneath the warm front. Warm air surged upward, then hit back with booming thunder and jagged spears of horizontal lightning. Rain tumbled loose and fell in driving curtains onto Grand Forks, then raced southward. In its path, trees bent in Nielsville, trash cans tumbled in Hendrum, a child's plastic tricycle clattered across an intersection in Fargo. Cars waited at both red and green lights in swirling rain.

Rocked backward by the lightning and rain, the cold front swirled, then drove harder underneath the humid wall. The warm front staggered backward five miles into western Minnesota, almost to Glyndon. Trees turned silvery as their leaves flipped upside down and shuddered

against their thin stems. Cows turned their rear ends to
the west as waves of cool rain washed over their backs. A
house under construction near Detroit Lakes lost its roof-
ing paper—which tore away in black sheets and swirled
into a nearby alfalfa field.

Rain began to fall on Alexandria, St. Cloud, and
Princeton—then curl northwest toward North Central
Speedway at Brainerd. Promoters and drivers and crew
chiefs huddled over their laptops to look at online
weather radar. The big green fishhook of precipitation
slowly bent and tightened around the heart of Minnesota.
The center of the weather had orange and red splotches—
heavy rain—with the main part of the front just east of
Fargo. The only area clear for Saturday night racing—at
least for now—was Headwaters Speedway.

Saturday

6:00 P.M.

That afternoon she took several calls from drivers and race teams in western and central Minnesota. Their first question: "Is it raining up there?"

"No. It's sunny and eighty-five degrees." Well, mostly sunny. All right, partly cloudy and so humid the back of her T-shirt stuck to her skin, but it was not raining. A couple of callers from across the border asked if it was raining *down* there. Southern Manitoba had thunderstorms, too.

"But you're racing tonight?"

"Racing tonight? Sure are. Sorry—it's a little loud here with all the cars," Mel replied, making sure her cell phone was turned toward the nearest revving engine.

"You're positive it's not gonna rain?" they persisted.

"I talked to the flight service people at Princeton, and they say we've got at least five hours of clear skies." (Actually, three to five hours, they had said, so it wasn't an outright lie.) "If you want to race tonight—if you're looking for points—Headwaters is where it's at."

The points thing closed the deal. Like NASCAR, the smaller WISSOTA organization—short for Wisconsin, Minnesota, North Dakota, South Dakota, northern Iowa, Wyoming, Montana, Manitoba, and Ontario—awarded drivers points just for showing up. Drivers received more points for placing and still more for winning. All race teams obsessed on their seasonal points accumulations. Just mentioning points was sort of like asking a boy if he'd like to get some coffee after school—it was almost too easy.

Now, from the announcer's booth, she paused to watch race cars and trailers roll in. Sonny Down Wind and his red and black No. 66 rolled along pit row. His car rode on an open trailer—made by Sonny himself. Sonny had a thing about doing all his own work. Bigger-budget sponsored teams had enclosed trailers and shiny pickups to pull them. The high-dollar Late Model crews came in motor homes that pulled professional racing trailers. For the first time ever, there was a long line of racing teams at the pit gate.

In the air above the scene came a flash of white: an osprey gliding in clutching a small fish. It was the female. Her family did their usual dance and chirp. The birds had the best seats at the speedway, and for a second, Mel saw it from their eyes: a square of thirty acres with the almost round eyeball of the racetrack dead center. Woods fronted three sides of the speedway grounds. A two-lane blacktop highway bordered the east side; an auto salvage yard lay just across the highway, and its snaking, overgrown rows of wrecked cars stretched like tentacles. Off the highway was the main gate and parking lot for fans, and beyond it the "back gate" entrance to the pit area. Pit row curved like an eyebrow around the top of the oval racetrack. Race teams and their colored cars and support vehicles gathered like colored pencil lines, like glitter above a single open eye.

"Quite a sight," remarked Art the announcer.

"For sure," Mel murmured. She lifted her binoculars for a closer look at the pits. Pit areas had their own crazy order. Local drivers used the backdrop signs as markers for their car groups, their classes. Out-of-town teams parked accordingly. Centered on "Dave's Pizza" at the far end were Late Models with their sleek, low, aerodynamic lines and long front ends like outstretched horses' necks. Shiny RV trailers parked behind them, their satellite dishes cupping the sky, their air conditioners humming. In front of "Mike's Quality Cars" were the Modifieds, with their fenderless front wheels and squatter bodies— workhorses rather than quarter horses. Smaller trailers and older RVs were the rule here. Near "Jim's Well and Septic" were the Super Stocks, with their manufactured plastic noses and rooflines, and their camper-trailer support vehicles parked behind.

Adjusting the focus for a closer look, she inched her glasses past the water tank on stilts where George filled

the tanker. Past the old road grader and a couple of ancient tow trucks overgrown with weeds and small trees
(those wrecks had to go!). Past the fueling area and its red
gasoline tanks roped off for safety—until she found the
Street Stocks and Pure Stocks. She looked for yellow
No. 32.

Trace usually parked below the "Palace Casino" bill-
board, but he had been pushed farther down the line by
the large number of race cars. She zoomed in closer.
Standing in his black racing suit, top down and its sleeves
tied around his waist, Trace leaned over his car. Both
hands on the fender, he stared down at the engine. He
didn't seem happy. Her eyes lingered on his backside.
Maybe it was the snug, zip-up, one-piece racing suits—
maybe that was what she liked about drivers.

She quickly moved her binoculars along the remainder
of pit row. To the left of Street and Pure Stocks were the
cute, boxy Mod-Fours. They were chassis-built just for
racing, with squared-off rear ends and shorter wheelbases.
And finally, lowest on the pecking order, were the battered Mini-Stocks and Pure Stocks of local racers. At this
end of the parking spectrum were small camper-trailers
and old school buses that doubled as living quarters, tool
shops, and towing vehicles. Tents poked up like mush-
rooms. Smoke wafted from grilling kettles.

Mel lowered her binoculars and took in the full scene.
Headwaters looked like a real racetrack. She had a surge of
hope—goose bumps rippled down her arms. She lifted her

glasses for one more quick look at Trace. At his square, wide shoulders and narrow waist.

"Mel!" said Maurice into her headset. "We need to start hot laps."

"Sorry. Say again?"

"I said, we're already fifteen minutes late on hot laps, and the weather's not going to hold off forever."

"Hang in there with me," Mel replied. "Dad's still checking in cars. I told the out-of-town Late Model teams we'd hold things for them."

"It sets a bad example," Maurice said. "It's unprofessional, plus the crowd will get restless."

"The crowd?" Mel said. "Look behind you, Maurice— the crowd's still coming in."

Maurice discreetly glanced over his shoulder (he'd once told Mel that a good flagman always faced frontward— never took his eyes off the track). He did a double take. Mel watched him stare at the throngs of people waiting to climb the bleachers. Those seated were squeezing together, moving their cushions and stadium chairs and blankets to make more room. Fans were digging out their protective eyewear against the dirt, their earplugs against the coming noise.

"This is our night, Maurice," Mel said, "the one we've been waiting for!"

"Maybe so," Maurice said, "but we can't have all these fans sitting here watching an empty track."

Beside Mel, Art Lempola nodded at that. He turned

down the country-western music and said into the microphone, "Ladies and gentlemen, I know you're waiting for a
big night of racing, and we'll get started soon." A retired
auctioneer with thinning hair and a sun-damaged face
(he kept having spots removed), Art had been handling
announcing duties at Headwaters since the speedway
started, back in the 1970s. "But, friends, this is a very special night. Due to rainouts around the state, Headwaters
Speedway is the place to be. We are where it's at. Look at
all those cars still checking in. You're going to witness history tonight here at Headwaters Speedway!"

There was scattered applause.

"We have enough cars in all the classes to run heat
races, then line up our features accordingly. However, because of the weather, we're going to do hot laps so they
can air out their engines and test their setups—then go
right to feature racing!"

More applause.

"I know for a fact," Art said, lowering his voice for effect, "that some of these boys have been up all night and
driving all day just to race here at Headwaters. So let's give
them time to get those cars checked in, checked out, and
set up right!"

There was more applause.

"The pill drawing," Mel murmured.

Art nodded. "Would all drivers gather at the pit area
gate for the feature race placement drawing? All drivers or
their representatives to the gate for the drawing, please."

He punched a button on the small CD player, and country music—Jim Reeves—began to play again through the loudspeakers.

Mel gave him a thumbs-up, not for his musical taste but for mentioning the drawing. There was no perfect way, other than qualifying heats—which took forever—to determine starting positions. Heat races also put the fastest cars up front. This made for boring, follow-the-leader races. Most dirt tracks used a lottery method to mix up the cars and force the faster cars to work their way through the pack. The result was a much better race—at least for the spectators. Drivers complained, but they complained about everything. They were always right there to draw their "pills," or numbers, from the pouch.

"So far, so good," Art murmured, hand over the microphone. "But we can't wait forever." He glanced at the sky.

Behind the booth, below the rear windows, the parking lot was nearly full. Patrick, the choir boy, stood just inside the gate and directed incoming traffic. He held an orange-nosed flashlight that he swung left and right; he was moving cars like a New York policeman during rush hour. She hoped he remembered to sing the national anthem.

"Right after the drawing, let's get the Mini-Stocks out there, and after them the Mod-Fours, Street and Pure Stocks," she said, turning back to the track. "All of the out-of-towners are Late Models and Super Stockers. That will give Cal Hopkins and those guys some breathing room."

"Cal Hopkins? Cal Hopkins is here?" Art said, turning to Mel.

Mel smiled.

"Holy moly," Art said. "Any chance we could we get him to step out and wave at the crowd?"

Mel paged her father, and within five minutes, the short, silvery-haired, silver-suited figure of Cal Hopkins was perched on the back of Johnny's ATV and headed down pit row.

"Ladies and gentlemen," Art said dramatically, "I have a major announcement."

The crowd quieted.

"If you direct your attention to pit row, you'll see what I mean by a 'special night.' Escorted onto the track by our track owner, Johnny Walters, is a special guest. Former sprint car champion, current national points leader in Late Model class, driver of the *Dirt World* green No. 42, please welcome"—Art paused for effect—"Cal Hopkins!"

Much of the crowd surged to their feet and let out a surprised roar.

"Take your time, Dad," Mel murmured and sucked in a breath. Johnny sped around the track with Cal waving with one hand and hanging on for his life with the other.

JOHNNY

"Thanks, Cal," Johnny said over his shoulder as they arrived back in the pits.

"No problem," Cal said, hopping off the ATV.

The two men searched for something more to say. Behind them, on the track, the Mini-Stocks finished their hot laps under Maurice's white flag.

"Looks like a big night for you," Cal said, his gaze following Johnny's.

"Yeah, looks that way." Johnny glanced at the pits, then across to the stands.

"Back gate looks good, front gate, too," Cal said.

Johnny's gaze swung to Cal. His eyes went to his name stitched black on silver on his racing suit, then flickered all the way down to his soft-soled, fire-resistant shoes.

"How's your season been going so far?" Cal asked, as if to fill the moment of dead air.

Johnny glanced away—at the sky—then back. "Good if I were farming."

Cal nodded. "Lots of rainouts all over this summer."

There was more awkward silence. In the middle of it, Sonny Down Wind rolled up in his Pure Stock and braked hard. He leaned out his window. "Hey, Johnny, you seen that worthless nephew of mine, Leonard?"

"No, I haven't," Johnny said.

"Well, if you do, tell him to get his butt in gear."

"Will do," Johnny said. He and Cal watched Sonny motor away. "Great driver," Johnny added. "Always in over his head, but he can find daylight better than anybody I've seen."

"I've seen you thread the needle more than a few times," Cal said.

Johnny shrugged. "But it just takes one mistake by somebody," he replied, and his voice trailed off.

Both men fell silent.

"So how are you doing, really?" Cal said. He focused his gaze on Johnny's face—a sure sign that he was trying not to look at Johnny's legs.

"Sally's long gone, I think you probably heard," Johnny said. "Remarried and lives in Ohio. Hooked up with some guy who has nothing to do with racing."

"I knew that," Cal said. "I should have—"

"Don't worry about it. I'm getting along fine. Me and my wheelchair and my ATV."

"And Melody," Cal said.

Johnny looked up with surprise.

"I talked to her on the phone. She called a bunch of us drivers. She's the reason we're all here."

Johnny allowed himself a smile. "She's a great kid—way smarter than me."

"My kids and Mary Lou live down in Kansas City," Cal said. "Have for five years or so."

"Sorry to hear that."

Cal shrugged. "Too many shows, too many late nights in the shop."

Johnny nodded.

Cal continued. " 'Who are you married to,' she asked me one night—'your racing team or me?' "

"I'd better let you go," Johnny said, glancing down pit row. "You've got things to do."

"It was the pause that did me in," Cal said.

Johnny looked at him.

"I hesitated for a split second before I answered 'You, honey,' " Cal said. "She was gone the next day."

Johnny was silent.

"Come by after the races—we'll catch up for real," Cal said.

Johnny hesitated. "If there's time," he said, and drove away.

BEAU

"Great," Beau muttered as he glanced down pit row. Approaching was a shiny tow truck from Joe's Westside Service. It pulled a covered trailer with Amber's car buttoned up inside.

"Please keep going, please keep going," Beau said, making sure he was busy with his car.

"Hi, Beau!" Amber called from the pickup. "Is there room here?"

"Not really," Beau said.

"I think we can squeeze in," Amber said.

"Why me?" Beau muttered as the Jenkins trailer began to back up.

"We could move," Jackster said.

"No, just ignore her," Dweeb said.

"A little late for that," Beau said. The Jenkinses' tow truck and shiny trailer loomed alongside Beau's car and crew like a semitrailer parking beside a Datsun. An image of Amber's red No. 13a was painted, full size, on the long trailer, and underneath it an advertisement for the brothers' gas station. Beau got his car to the speedway by the kindness of friends with pickups. Sometimes they scrounged a trailer, other times they had to tow the race car. In the racing world, towing your car to the track was the equivalent of being homeless. It was like standing at a stoplight with a cardboard sign that read, "Will race for gas and tires."

Guitar Hero watched as the Jenkins family, with their matching red shirts and caps, began to unload. "They could be, like, a real pit crew," he said.

"They *are* a real pit crew, you idiot," Beau said.

"Hey," Amber called to Beau with a chin-jerk to Guitar Hero—whose face always lit up at the sight of Amber and her curly red hair; now his jaw moved, but no words came out.

"Ninth-grade boys are so pitiful," Beau remarked.

"He's going to pee his pants," Dweeb said. The pit area was loud enough that they didn't have to whisper—not that Guitar Hero would have heard them.

"But here's the really sad part," Jackster said to Beau. "You're the one she likes."

"Yeah, right!" Beau said, and bent over his engine.

"It's true," Dweeb said. "Amber just doesn't have any girlie skills. At the moment, parking next to you is all she's got."

Jackster nodded at this wisdom.

"R-racing tonight?" Guitar Hero stammered to Amber.

"No," Beau said, mimicking Amber's voice, "just showing off my fully sponsored car and meathead crew of brothers, all of whom are real mechanics, unlike you losers."

"Whatcha workin' on?" Amber asked, stepping closer to Beau.

"The brakes," Beau said, his fingers on the carburetor.

Dweeb and Jackster giggled.

Amber blinked; she didn't get the joke.

"Looks like you might have some competition tonight," Beau said, glancing down the lineup of about twenty Mod-Fours, half of which were from out of town.

Amber surveyed the other racers, then shrugged.

"Nothing you can't handle, right?" Beau said.

"We know the track, they don't," Amber replied. "It'll take them half the race to figure out that soft spot in turn 1."

"Yeah, well, good drivers catch on fast."

"True," Amber said, "but I ain't worried." As she checked out the other teams, her back straightened, her

shoulders squared. Beau hated to say it, but she was one of
the few natural drivers out here. Like Sonny Down Wind,
she never overthought things. She just drove fast.

Amber turned back and eyeballed No. 19z. "What's
this, your good luck charm?" She reached out to Beau's little sock monkey, which was tied to the roll cage.

"Never touch the monkey!" Beau said, jumping in
front of her.

Dweeb and Jackster broke up. Amber only drew back
her hand and leaned sideways to look around him.

"He's cute. Your mom make him?"

"No, I did," Beau said sarcastically.

"Really?" Amber said, her round, freckled face opening
into a smile. She had a full, wide mouth, and there was a
slight gap between her front teeth.

"No, not really," Beau said, rolling his eyes.

A hurt look flickered across Amber's face.

"Don't mind him," Guitar Hero said quickly. "He's always intense just before hot laps."

Beau looked over her shoulder as one of Amber's
brothers rolled her car backward down the trailer's ramp.
He squinted. "What happened to your tin?"

"Long story," Amber said.

"Looks like a crazy person attacked it with a welder,"
Dweeb said.

Amber was silent.

Just then Beau noticed another Jenkins brother still in
the tow truck. He wore wraparound sunglasses and was

hunched low in the cab as he peered out at the racetrack, at the people and cars. Beau jabbed Dweeb with an elbow and nodded toward the truck.

"Lance," Amber said. "He got the bright idea that I needed armor plating."

They all stared. Lance looked their way, then ducked out of sight.

"Sorry," Dweeb said quickly.

"It's all right," Amber said. "We got the steel off, and we got him to come along to the races—first time since he got hurt—so it's all good."

Beau nodded. "Luck tonight," he said. It was the least he could do.

" 'Luck'?" Amber asked. "That could go either way—good luck, bad luck."

"You hardly ever need good luck," he said, with a brief glance into her green eyes.

"Thanks—I think," Amber said with a smile, and turned back to her car.

Beau's gaze fell down her snug red racing suit, tight across her buns, and down her strong thighs and rounded calves. He shook his head to clear it. Reaching up to his sock monkey, he adjusted the little fellow's tail. It was wrapped twice around the tubing. The monkey was the ultimate in cute—and the perfect disguise for the new welding of his own on the upper roll cage.

Guitar Hero came close to inspect the cage. "I still say—"

"Hey, it's welded, all right?" Beau said. "Make yourself useful and check the tire pressure. Twelve pounds, max."

AMBER

She swung herself feetfirst through the side window and into the cockpit. Her brothers adjusted her seat belt, tugged on her shoulder harness. Joe, Jimmy, and Ken fussed over her like, well, older brothers.

"No more than 7000 rpm during hot laps," Joe said, handing her the quick-release steering wheel.

"I know, I know," she said, locking it in place.

"And back off easy from that," he added.

"If you back it off too fast, the engine will wrap and throw a rod," Amber said in his voice.

"Okay, okay," Joe said. He actually smiled.

She flipped her toggle switch, then fired the engine. The four-cylinder exhaust header dumped a low, sweet growl from the left side of the engine. She watched her gauges until their needles came up.

"Good?" Joe asked, leaning his head into the cockpit.

"Good," Amber said.

Jimmy strapped on her neck restraint, made sure the steering wheel's nose pad was in place, then cinched her shoulder harness tighter.

"I need to breathe!" she protested.

"Sorry, kid," he said, loosening the shoulder harness but not by much. "Only got one little sister."

"Yeah, yeah," Amber said. Joe hooked her window net, then she pulled on her helmet and flipped down her visor to hide a smile. Beau was right; she was lucky already.

With a thumbs-up for her brothers, she blipped the throttle and turned onto pit row. Passing the other Mod-Four teams, she made a point of not looking at them—and spinning some dust and gravel their way as a little statement. Then it was up over the bank and onto the track, where she merged with other bright-colored Mod-Fours.

During a slow lap under Maurice's yellow, she watched her gauges, listened to her engine, and tried to get a feel for the dirt. Like the other drivers, she swung her car side to side to warm and loosen the front tires, getting a feel for their grip, and the moisture level in the dirt. Maurice soon pulled back the yellow, replacing it with a furled green flag. He leaned over his railing and waggled it, point up, like an unopened umbrella.

On the first hot lap, Amber knew she was not in Kansas anymore. The Mod-Fours from Fargo, Grand Forks, and western Minnesota bolted forward like a herd of wild ponies. She was not used to driving flat out during hot laps. At Headwaters, racing with the locals, she always saved something for later. Tonight she pushed her little Ford block to the limit, finding a good line medium-high, then diving low, especially in turns 2 and 3. The out-of-town drivers were older, aggressive, and they clearly had extra sheet metal in their trailers. Twice she got rocked by bump-and-run drivers—her right side aluminum skin screeched—but she didn't retaliate or start throwing the customary one-fingered salute. That she left to the boys. In auto racing, testosterone was not necessarily a good thing. She prided herself on the mental game—on strategy. Turn 1 had its notorious soft spot, which she could use to her advantage in the feature race, so she left it alone for now. Hot laps were not supposed to be actual racing, but she could not help battling the out-of-towners just a bit. She found a line down low and stayed there. Down low had no good line, but they didn't have to know that.

Beau in his mosquito-fogging pink and black No. 19z made a brief statement as he tried to get by on her high side. How his little car ran so well she could never figure out, but tonight he would be lucky to make the top fifteen. Around her the Fargo and Grand Forks cars hummed like bees ready to sting.

Well up in the pack, she grabbed a good middle line and found herself wheel to wheel with silver No. 55. Its black-helmeted driver lagged back for a half second in turn 1, then "accidentally" laid his car against her driver's side. The No. 55 car pushed her high—and close to the edge of the track, where there was no guardrail. He rode her toward the edge—she heard herself swear—letting her loose only at the last second.

Free from No. 55, she fought the instinct—as when a deer bounds across the highway—to overcorrect. To yank the wheel. Any sudden move, especially with the Mod-Four's steering quickener in place, would cause her to spin out—leave her sideways and open for a serious hit from another car. There were times to drive and times to trust the car. She loosened her gloved hands on the wheel. She took what little No. 13a gave her. Its rubber never lost its grip. The steering corrected itself, and Amber came out high and straight, well behind No. 55. She resisted the urge to chase him and stayed out of trouble until Maurice threw the white flag, signaling the end of hot laps.

Coasting into the pits, sheet metal flapping, Amber saw her brothers waiting—but not for her. As silver No. 55 came down pit row, Joe and Jimmy stepped out to flag the driver down.

Amber leaned out her window. "Don't!" she shouted. Ahead, No. 55 swerved sharply around her brothers and flashed them the one-fingered wave.

"Those were hot laps, you idiot!" Joe shouted, shaking his fist after the car.

Jimmy and Ken upped the ante with some choice comments of their own.

"It's all right, forget about it!" Amber called to them. She turned in sharply and parked.

"Who is that driver, anyway?" Joe asked, helping Amber through the window.

"Beats me," Amber said. She stood up straight and

pulled off her helmet. Her forehead and neck were sweaty already.

Lance leaned out of the tow truck. "He—he tried to wreck you!"

They all paused.

"Whoa," Joe whispered. They all looked at Lance.

"Well, he did!" Lance said. For the first time in a long while his voice sounded normal.

"Hey, Lance, not to worry," Amber said. She went over and put her hand on his arm. "Just part of racing. He'll get his."

"He should have been warned at least," Jimmy muttered as they bent to work on the tin. "I mean, jeez, this was only hot laps. What's he going to do in the feature?"

"Maybe Maurice will black-flag him," Ken said.

"Maurice won't black-flag any out-of-town cars," Joe said.

"Why's that?" Ken asked.

"Because he thinks we local yokels need to learn how to drive," Joe replied, glaring across the track.

Nobody really liked Maurice. "Maybe he's right," Amber said. "Maybe a little competition is a good thing." She shook out her red hair as Beau coasted in and killed his engine.

"Way to go, dude," Jackster called. "We who are allergic to mosquito bites thank you."

"My pleasure," Beau said, with a glance to Amber and her torn metal.

Amber strolled over to Beau's car.

"How'd you do in the drawing?"

Beau shrugged. "Thirteenth. Lucky me. You?"

"Fifth."

Beau had nothing to say.

"Some fast cars out there tonight," she said, brushing away a couple of red tendrils that curled down her forehead.

"Some dirty drivers, too," Dweeb said. "If No. 55 did that to me, I'd come back and nail him."

"And wreck your car," Amber said. Her green eyes gleamed.

"Hey—boys will be boys," Beau said. There was a long moment when he almost smiled at her.

"I was thinking," Amber said to him. "You should bring your car over to our shop sometime. We could go through your engine. It needs rings for sure, and when we've got it apart we could bore and hone your cylinders, too. My brothers love that sort of thing. They're always looking for a project."

"Is that what I am, a 'project'?" Beau asked.

Amber's face froze—then tightened around her eyes and mouth. "No, Beau, you're not a project," she said. "You're an ass."

TRACE

He solved the engine miss himself. It was, after all, the timing. The distributor cap was cockeyed—off by several degrees. Once he had repositioned the pole, yellow No. 32 ran fine. Or at least it sounded fine.

During warm-ups he goosed the gas pedal again and again as he swerved side to side to warm the tires. The overall setup—suspension, shocks, and tires—felt good, but there was some small, unnamed thing still not right with the engine. The rpm were there; the power was not.

To save time, the Street Stocks and Pure Stocks ran hot laps together. When Maurice threw the green, Trace dove down low and tried to find a good line through the corners. Trouble was, he kept seeing Sonny Down Wind's red and black No. 66 just off his right rear fender. Sonny was a great driver—maybe the best local racer—and did all his own engine work. That is, what was allowable under Pure Stock rules. Some people thought that Sonny had a few tricks up his sleeve engine-wise, such as some valve porting and head polishing. But for a Pure Stock to run even with a Street Stock was humiliating.

Trace tried a line higher on the bank—but when he came down, there was Sonny right on his door. Everybody's car had more horsepower on the straightaway. Gradually he fell back place by place. He lost track of the Street Stock leader, orange No. 27, from Grand Rapids, until the car surged by on Trace's right side. He had been lapped. Maurice waved the white flag to end hot laps, and Trace coasted into the pits fast and angry.

"What'sa matter out there?" his dad asked. "You were running almost last. Sonny Down Wind was right on your butt."

"Sonny's car runs right, this one doesn't!" Trace shot back. By the trailer, Larry looked through tools, trying to be inconspicuous.

Trace's dad held up both hands, palms out. "Is it set up wrong? How do the shocks and weight distribution feel?"

"It's set up fine," Trace said, pulling himself through the window. "The toe's right, the ride's just heavy enough. I'm telling you, it's the engine. The power is just not there." He glared at Larry.

"The engine is fine," Larry said, walking over. He leaned down and yanked the throttle linkage; the stock car's engine barked, then settled back into a smooth, throaty hum. "See?"

"Yeah, but there's no power at the high end," Trace said, rattling his helmet into the cockpit.

"Sure you were flat out?" Trace's dad asked.

"I had my foot through the damn floor!"

"Easy, easy," Mr. Bonham said.

Larry muttered something and spit to the side.

"What did you say?" Trace said, grabbing Larry by the arm.

Larry batted away Trace's hand. "I said, 'I don't think it's the engine.' "

"What do you think it is, then?" Trace asked, in his face now. "You tell me right now what you think it is."

Larry glanced at Don Bonham. "Maybe it's the driver."

"Maybe we could get somebody else to look at it before the feature," Don said quickly—and stepped between Larry and Trace. "Get a second opinion."

"That's a damn good idea," Trace said.

"No need for that. I'll go over it again," Larry said quickly. "There could be something I missed."

Trace and his father both looked at Larry.

"All right," Don said. "Take another look." He avoided eye contact with Trace and turned to check his Black-Berry.

"Dad," Trace began. He grabbed his father's arm and pulled him away from Larry so they could talk.

"It's all right," his father said. "It's just racing."

"No, it's not all right." Trace paused, looked out at the track. "Maybe it's me. Maybe I am a lousy driver. Maybe I just don't have it."

His father was silent. Then he said, "You've got lots of skills in lots of areas, Trace. You're going to do fine in life. Not everybody's cut out to be a driver."

PATRICK

George himself promoted Patrick to pit duty. Because of all the extra cars, Patrick was assigned to drive the speedway's push truck, a battered, rusted three-quarter-ton Dodge Power Wagon with homemade oak-wood bumpers padded with strips of tire rubber. It was a beast—the manual transmission cruder than the wrecker's. Patrick practiced a few runs in the far corner of the pit area until he got the hang of the big pedals.

Easing down pit row, looking for any car that needed a rolling start on its way to hot laps, Patrick saw Trace Bonham. In a black racing suit, he was standing alone and stiff, his arms crossed over his chest. For some weird reason he was looking off toward the trees. Alongside him, a beefy guy with his butt crack on display was bent over the open engine compartment of Trace's car.

Patrick lurched to a stop and leaned out his window.

"Hey, Trace."

Trace turned to stare at him.

"It's me. Patrick. From school?"

Trace continued to stare. Patrick felt like he was speaking Russian.

"You need a push?"

"A push?" Trace replied.

"That's what I do. Drive the push truck," Patrick said.

"Do I need a push!" Trace repeated, stepping forward. His face was red and blotchy.

Patrick shrank backward into the cab. "Sorry!" he said, and threw the truck in gear.

"No, wait!" Trace said.

As Trace approached, Patrick remained ready to accelerate.

"It's not you, man. Sorry. I didn't recognize you for a second. And no, I don't need a push. What I need is— I don't know what I need! A new crew chief. A new engine. One or the other." Without asking, Trace went around, yanked open the door, kicked garbage aside, and slumped in the old truck's passenger seat. He stared through the windshield down pit row.

Patrick had no idea of what to say.

"First it was the timing—which I fixed," Trace said. "Now Larry's looking at the carburetor—which I already checked out. You know what I really think?" Trace asked, turning to Patrick; he had a crazy look in his eyes.

"What do you really think?" Patrick asked. His hand felt for the door handle in case he had to exit, stage left.

"He's sabotaging me."

"Who?" Patrick said.

"Larry, my crew chief," Trace said, pointing back to the yellow car. His face flushed redder. "That guy right there. He hates me. 'Rich kid—why should *he* get to drive?'" Trace said in another voice. "'I had to *work* my way up.'"

"Sabotage, whoa," Patrick said, keeping his hand on the door handle.

Trace turned to Patrick. "It's all there, don't you see? It's just a question of finding out how he does it."

Patrick glanced again at Butt Crack Larry.

Trace's gaze followed his. "I've got an idea," he said suddenly. He turned to Patrick. "You know anything about cars?"

"Not really," Patrick said with an apologetic shrug.

"Doesn't matter," Trace said. "What I need you to do is watch him."

"Watch him?"

"Yes, him." Trace jerked his chin toward Larry.

"You mean, like spy on him?"

"Exactly," Trace said. "See if he does anything strange to the car."

"How will I know if it's strange?"

"I'll know if it's strange," Trace said. "All you have to do is keep an eye on him. Tell me everything he does."

"I'll try," Patrick said. "I could park over there by the track entrance and watch him through my mirror. I'm supposed to hang there anyway with the push truck."

"Great!" Trace said, and punched Patrick on the shoulder.

Patrick winced and tried not to rub his arm.

Trace got out. He blinked, seemed to place Patrick for real this time. "Hey—you doing the anthem tonight?"

"Yes."

Trace nodded. "I always wished I could sing."

TUDY

Ritchie was humming like crazy. He either hummed or talked nonstop when he was working. Once he stepped into the steamy pork breath of the wagon, he came alive. Woke up. "Hey, Bob!" and "What say, Jay?" he called to the customers lined up, many of whom Tudy recognized. If anything, Ritchie's customers were loyal. He could talk to them and make pork sandwiches without looking at his hands. Tudy, slumped onto a tall stool, ran the cash register. Behind her, Leonard sat in a folding chair with an ice bag held to the back of his head.

"My brain's going to freeze," he said to Winona in his soft lilt.

Tudy giggled.

"A few more minutes of ice will make your headache go away," Winona said.

"It feels like my whole head has gone away," Leonard said.

Tudy giggled again.

"Say, didn't I give you a ten?" a customer, an old geezer, said loudly.

"Yes. Sorry!" she said, and made correct change.

"Has Sonny got anybody else to help him crew tonight?" Ritchie said.

"I don't think so," Leonard said. "Maybe I should go back." He stood up, then winced—keeping one eye on Tudy.

"You sit right back down," Winona said. "You took a blow to the head, so you should stay quiet. That's why Sonny sent you over. When your headache's gone, you can help us here."

"But what about Sonny?" Leonard began.

"Sonny's fine. There are all sorts of boys—and girls, too—who'll help him. And if he complains about your being gone, he won't get any fry bread after the race."

Leonard maintained his pained look. As Tudy returned to running the till, she could feel him watching her. The small of her back was damp with sweat; a gray blossom grew on her white blouse, and her arms glistened. She kept tugging at the front of her blouse to fan air down there.

THE WEATHER

The giant bowl of warm, moist air moved slowly eastward on a curving line from Winnipeg, Manitoba, to Spring Grove, Minnesota, in the southeastern corner of the state. Pushed and probed by the cold front, it threw back wind and lightning—and rain.

Clouds burst open. Rain dumped on the rich farmland of northwestern Minnesota. Muddy runoff gathered in field tiling, pipes dug into low-lying sections for relief from this kind of storm. The outlet pipes began to spout leg-thick geysers of water into ditches. Dark, coffee-colored flow slid along roads at fast walking speed. The runoff carried ditch trash: white foam coffee cups, blue beer cans, green two-liter Mountain Dew bottles, a broken pine board.

In the small towns, the rain battered shop windows and parked cars, cleaning dust from the fenders and mud from the tires of farm pickups like a giant, free car wash. Farther south and east, into pine and lake country, the leading edge of the front whipped at the trees. Pine tops snapped and sailed twenty yards downwind. Birds braced against the sides of their nests and tried to cover their chicks with their outstretched wings. The rain and wind rolled eastward.

The sky in Thief River Falls, Hawley, and Pelican Rapids turned from gray to yellowish. The air was still and rainless. Even little kids on their bikes knew enough to head for home.

As the warm front gave way, the cold front rammed harder underneath and picked up speed. The leading edge of cold wind and rain quickened its pace from ten to twenty-five miles per hour. That speed put it on pace to hit Headwaters Speedway in three hours. Give or take. Not that the weather cared.

Saturday
8:00 P.M.

MAURICE

After hot laps, Maurice had several cars on his "watch list." They included the silver No. 55 in the Mod-Four class, the orange No. 27 Street Stock, plus a couple of local Late Models whose drivers were clearly gunning for Cal Hopkins. Not that Cal Hopkins couldn't take care of himself. However, there were two types of drivers: those who just liked to go fast, and those who tried to keep others from going fast.

The first category of drivers, such as Hopkins, kept their eyes on the prize. That meant finishing the race, finishing as high up as they could, and not wrecking their cars. They scored their points in the standings, not during the race by running over somebody. The second type of driver was too aggressive, held grudges, caused spinouts and crashes—which brought out Maurice's yellow flag. The crowd hated restarts. Restarts caused delays, and tonight of all nights there was little margin for that.

"Okay, Maurice, let's get Patrick up there," came Mel's voice.

After making sure his flags were secure, Maurice gave up his little white-fenced pen to Patrick, the high school kid with the silvery voice and nice jeans and boots. Patrick readied himself with the handheld microphone.

"Ladies and gentlemen," Art Lempola intoned gravely, "please direct your attention to the pit entrance. Entering the track, driving in staggered order, are three cars. Each is carrying a different flag. First is our own Old Glory, driven by Late Model Champion John Sitz. Next, the Maple Leaf of our Great Neighbor to the north, driven by Elliot Arnason. And trailing, the colors of the mighty Red Lake Nation, driven by Sonny Down Wind. Please rise— and, men, be sure to remove your caps!"

The rustling, the thudding of hundreds of boots and shoes on the boards, never failed to bring goose bumps to Maurice's forearms.

"Oh, say can you see . . ." began Patrick in a high Irish tenor as the colors slowly circled the track. The flagman flashed back to Navy days when the ship came in: the men in orderly rows with their clean white uniforms, the colored flags, the band and the crowd waiting onshore.

He glanced into the stands. A couple of grown men had forgotten to remove their caps. Kids old enough to know better were horsing around and not paying attention. Less than half of the crowd stood in the correct, right-hand-over-heart position. On the other hand, people were here at the speedway. They had left their television sets and their couches. Friends. Strangers. Townspeople, farmers, kids, Natives from the local reservations—they were all here, packed tightly in the bleachers. This was the beauty of small-town Saturday night racing.

"And now, as a salute to our friends across the border, the Canadian national anthem."

Patrick slid into "O Canada." As anthems went, the Canadian one was much easier to sing than "The Star-Spangled Banner." Maurice knew the words, but he only hummed along. He was a patriotic American. He did not fully approve of singing the Canadian anthem at American sporting events—or, for that matter, all the hullabaloo about the Red Lake "nation." But a professional flagman, like a referee, did not call attention to himself or make political statements. He was there to run the race. Period.

As Patrick finished, the crowd cheered and stamped its collective feet. The bleachers thundered and those goose bumps came back.

"Great job," Maurice said to Patrick.

The boy blushed, then clumsily shook hands with Maurice and waved briefly to the crowd.

"And now, let's . . . go . . . racing!" Art boomed from the loudspeakers.

Fifteen Mini-Stocks streamed onto the track. Maurice hurried back to his pen to greet them, green flag ready when they were—and not until then.

GEORGE

As he watched the Mini-Stocks, George was embarrassed. Not for them, the unsponsored, battered local cars straining down the straightaway and making more noise than speed, but because of the dust. The track was turning into a dirt slick. Contrails of fine brown dirt streamed behind the cars, then curled upward into the humid air. With each lap, the dust slowly gathered itself and hung above the infield like a thin brown mushroom cloud. The osprey nest shrank in the haze. A breeze to clear the air would have been perfect—but with wind would come weather.

In the Pure Stock class, with Sonny Down Wind working his way through the pack, the dust worsened. It was a miracle that Sonny could see anything, let alone an open seam. Cars farther back were completely out of sight in the rolling brown haze.

"George, it's getting dusty out there." Mel's voice crackled in his headset.

"I know, I know."

"How much did you water this afternoon?"

"Not enough, clearly," George said. "The water truck ain't doing so well."

"What's the trouble?"

"The valves suck. I mean, for real. The engine's losing compression. I thought we could get through the summer, but now I'm not sure we can get through tonight."

There was a pause. "Now you tell me, George," Mel said.

"With the weather and all, I figured you and Johnny had enough to worry about," George said. "I was going to go through the engine myself this winter and—"

"Okay, okay, George. What about tonight?"

"The truck is good for two or three more laps at most. If we're lucky, we can water one more time."

There was silence in his earphones. George could feel Mel's mind clicking through their options. He could see her long fingers drumming as she thought. On the track, Sonny Down Wind was cruising—poised to lap the trailing car.

"Let's save the water for the Mod-Fours and Late Models," Mel said. "And if the truck dies out there, don't worry about it. Have Patrick ready in the wrecker to pull you off the track."

Coming out of turn 2, Sonny Down Wind's red and black No. 66 went up in smoke. A blue contrail spewed from underneath his Chevy.

"Dang it!" George said.

"What now?" Mel said instantly.

"Sorry. Just watching Sonny. Something let loose in his engine," George said.

Mel was silent a moment. "Doesn't look good," she agreed.

Sonny coasted up high, then cranked the wheel, taking him over the top and down into the pits toward George.

"That engine's toast," George said to Mel. "I can hear it rattling. Pistons must have swapped holes, or else he threw a rod."

"Now maybe he'll let somebody sponsor him," Mel said.

"Don't bet on it," George said.

PATRICK

After nailing the anthems, Patrick returned to push truck and spy duty. He slouched in the smelly cab, the brim of his baseball cap pulled low on his forehead. Trace's yellow No. 32 was centered in his cracked rearview mirror. Patrick had worked in retail one summer, at a men's clothing store in the mall, and Larry fit the profile of a shoplifter. He lingered near the car. He picked tools up. He put them down. Kicked the tires. Pretended to check their pressure. On the other hand, he was the crew chief.

Trace spoke briefly to Larry, then headed down pit row to the line of portable toilets. As he walked away, Trace sneaked a glance at Patrick. Patrick gave him the briefest of nods, then returned to his surveillance. Larry waited until Trace was gone. Then, glancing around to make sure that Don Bonham was also occupied, he went to the rear of the car. He carried what looked to be a long screwdriver. Quickly loosening the trunk lid fasteners, he leaned in over the fuel cell. Whatever he did took about five seconds. Then Larry refastened the tin deck and put away the screwdriver.

Patrick fired up the push truck and headed down to the toilets. He waited there, feeling a little strange about watching the toilet doors, but soon enough Trace emerged, zipping up his racing suit. Patrick tooted the horn; Trace hurried over.

"I don't know if this means anything," Patrick began, and described Larry's movements.

Trace's face got a blank look as he thought. "The only thing back there is the fuel cell," he said, as if talking to himself. "And fuel line." Suddenly he grabbed Patrick by the shirt. "That SOB!" he blurted.

"Easy, Trace!" Patrick said, pulling back.

"Patrick—we need a push on turn 3!" Mel's voice crackled in his headset. "If you'll notice, one of the Pure Stocks died out there."

"Sorry, Mel!" he said quickly. "I'm helping Trace and—"

"Trace doesn't need your help. I do!"

"I'm on it," he said. "Gotta go," he said to Trace, but Trace was already gone. Patrick dropped the clutch pedal and lurched the truck down pit row.

On the track, he drove quickly toward the stalled car. The best push truck drivers braked at the last moment, slowing to a sweet, soft bumper-to-bumper kiss. But haze and dust threw off Patrick's depth of field. As he drew near, the stalled car grew way larger way faster than it should have. He jammed on the brakes—was mostly stopped—but crashed into the stalled car. The battered Pure Stock slammed forward as if it had been rear-ended at a stop sign. The driver stuck out his arm and shook his fist at Patrick. The crowd let out a rolling laugh followed by loud clapping.

"I said a push. I didn't say break his neck," Mel squawked.

"Sorry," Patrick mumbled into his little microphone.

Luckily the Pure Stock already had a smashed rear end, so another bumper crunching was not a big deal. Soon enough the driver's engine coughed and fired. The beat-up stock car pulled away and sped around to catch up with the others for the rolling restart. As Patrick drove past the stands on his way to the pits, the crowd gave him a standing ovation.

"Great," Patrick muttered, forgetting that his mic was on.

He heard a giggle in his ears. "They love you, Patrick," Mel said.

"Yeah, well . . ." Patrick trailed off.

"Hey, nice singing by the way," Mel said.

"Thanks. Say, Mel, you want to get a barbecue or something after the races?"

"Patrick—don't miss the pit entrance this time," she interrupted—but she didn't say no.

Turning onto pit row, driving on cloud ten, Patrick almost ran over two guys rolling in the dirt, whaling away at each other. It was Trace and Larry, slugging it out.

TRACE

In the twenty-lap feature, he was going to eat dust—but not for long. Starting in the next-to-last row among the Street Stocks, Trace blipped the throttle again and again. Funny how well an engine ran without a hose clamp pinching the fuel line.

At first he suspected that Larry had installed the fuel "log," or filter, backward. That would have been enough to starve the engine at full throttle. But the sabotage was way simpler: a small metal hose clamp on the half-inch-diameter flexible fuel line. For safety reasons, once it was beyond the fire wall, the fuel line ran through a metal conduit—a hose within a steel pipe. This prevented fuel leaks and fires inside the cockpit. But between the fuel cell and the rear fire wall, flexible hose was legal. Larry had placed a hose clamp right where the flex line entered the conduit. A quick quarter turn with a Phillips-head screwdriver, and the noose tightened. Larry had not pinched the line fully shut—that way the engine wouldn't have run at all—but just enough to retard full gas flow. The two-barrel Holley carburetor was rated at 500 cfm. Larry's little pinch job left its flow at around 450—a guess on Trace's part—but clearly enough to take away his top-end horse-power.

He slammed his gloved hands on the wheel in anger—then winced. His knuckles were scraped. So was the side of his face. But Larry was gone. Larry was history! Other drivers had rushed over to stop the fight. When they separated Larry and Trace, Trace had told them about the hose clamp. "I told you it wasn't running right!" he shouted at his father as two men held him back.

"What's going on here!" Johnny Walters demanded, skidding to a stop on his ATV. "You know the rules about fighting!"

Trace repeated his accusation.

"You men keep them separated. We'll take a look," Johnny said. He and Don Bonham went to the rear of yellow No. 32 and examined the fuel line.

"A hose clamp painted the same color as the fuel line," Johnny announced. All the men turned toward Larry.

There was silence.

"Why did you do it, Larry?" Don asked.

Larry shrugged and spit to the side.

Suddenly Don was in his face. "I'm asking you, Larry—why'd you sandbag my son?"

"Easy, Don!" Johnny Walters called. He accelerated his four-wheeler alongside and with his Popeye right arm pulled Don back.

"Kid don't deserve a ride like this," Larry said. "Me, I had to work my way up. Nobody handed me anything."

"Well, you're gonna have to work your way up somewhere else," Don said. "Your ass is fired. I want you out of here!"

"I'll second that," Johnny said. "We don't tolerate cheaters of any kind at this track. Larry, you've got five minutes to get gone."

"We'll make sure of that!" said a burly crew guy. Other men muttered their agreement and stepped up to surround Larry. The group of them walked him to his truck. He jumped inside, slammed the door, and turned the key. The engine didn't start immediately.

"Fuel line problems?" someone hollered; there were catcalls. Larry bent forward in the cab and cranked the starter until the engine caught—then accelerated away.

Now Trace had to focus on driving. "Yahoo 32!" he shouted inside his helmet, but his jaw hurt, too. In the rule book there was a fine for fighting—but he would have to worry about that later.

Ahead, the lead drivers dropped the hammer: green flag. Trace stamped his right foot down as well. His exhaust headers let loose a deep, throaty roar. Full power for the first time all season! However, as he thundered past the flag stand, he was also careful not to overdo it—certainly not in turn 1 of lap 1. For drivers, the first turn after green was like high school kids bolting for the classroom door when the lunch bell rang. Somebody always got knocked down. Ahead, several cars traded paint. Two bumped tires and flashed undercarriages—almost flipping over—but they slammed back onto dirt without spinning out. Trace snaked between them to pick up four places.

He pressed hard, drove smart. Turn 1's soft spot was to no one's advantage. Everybody seemed to know about the soft spot. The dust—thick and rolling—was also the same for everyone except the leader, orange No. 27. Trace found a higher line where he could see better—he caught flashes of orange No. 27—but up high the track was longer, and he made up no ground.

In laps 4 and 5, he tried more of a "diamond" line— drive hard in the apex of the turn, break loose the rear end, swing it to the inside, then accelerate out on a sharp angle. He had plenty of power. Still, he made up little ground. By lap 8, he knew what he had to do: get down in the dust with the other cars and drive like God loved him.

By lap 12, he ran in the middle of the pack. Lap by lap, one by one, he picked off the cars in front of him. He gambled low and gained one more place. Gambled high in turn 4 and made up one more. It was like driving in a dust storm—visibility one car length—at eighty miles an hour. Drive flat out and hope that there wasn't a logging truck stalled on the road. By lap 15, he was running third.

The leader, orange No. 27, had the advantage of slightly better visibility. But leaders usually suffered from "look-back" syndrome—as in "Don't look back, they might be gaining." From the few times he had led a race, Trace knew how easy it was to get focused backward rather than forward. Swerving left, then right, then back, he gradually got their attention. The front two cars began to tighten up. Not tighten up as in closer together, but tighten up in the sense of squeezing it—like a pitcher squeezing the baseball and starting to lose his strike zone. They were thinking too much. Getting out of sync. By lap 17, he was inside their heads. He was reading their minds: "Two laps to go. That yellow No. 32's got a lot of horse-power. He's going to make a move. I just know he's going to make a move!"

Under the white flag—one more lap—he went for it. The leaders were two wide in turn 2, battling it out on a medium-low line. They had positions 1 and 2 locked up—in their minds. This left a seam down low—really low—where the track turned into the infield, and the clay was chunky and bone dry. Seeing a half car length of open space, Trace made his move. He cranked the wheel left and dove down. Orange No. 27, focused on the second-place car, saw him too late. Trace was almost even with the guy's door when the driver of orange No. 27 pinched him—tried to run Trace off the track and into the white bumper tires, which suddenly looked as big as logging trucks. Trace pinched back. He cranked yellow No. 32 against the side of orange No. 27. Metal grated. Tires touched and smoked. The two cars drifted higher, jostling the third car—whose driver lost his nerve and dropped back. Trace and orange No. 27 split apart down the straightaway and went flat out side by side. Neither gained a foot on the other. Approaching turn 3, it was a question which driver would go deepest into the corner. It was a classic game of chicken: who would hold the pedal down the longest?

Deep in the turn, still flat out, Trace took his car's right front tire, its tie-rod and shock absorber to the breaking point. Centrifugal force hung him forward in his shoulder harness. He gained a third of a car length on orange No. 27. But there was still turn 4, which had to be navigated cleanly in order to make a run at the checkered. Orange No. 27 bumped his right side—Trace fought the wheel to keep his line—and the two cars rocked each other out of turn 4 and all the way through the checkered flag.

Which Trace barely saw. Because of the dust and the battle with No. 27, he did not know who won. He slowed alongside the orange car. Its driver held up his hands in a questioning gesture. Trace shrugged as well. He pointed forward. The other driver flashed a thumbs-up. Together, at yellow-flag pace, orange No. 27 and Trace's No. 32 came around again, side by side, toward the flag stand and the appreciative fans.

Maurice continued to swirl the checkered flag in a slow, wide figure-eight motion. The crowd remained standing and clapping. Trace looked briefly around his car for the source of the dull thumping noise—he thought he had a flat tire or a bent rim—then realized it was fans stamping their feet on the boards.

Maurice teased the drivers, letting them approach

closer and closer—then suddenly bent low over his railing and pointed the checkered flag at Trace.

"Yes!" Trace shouted. He pounded his wheel and let out a whoop that he had been holding in for a long time. Before taking a victory lap, he remembered to turn onto the infield and get weighed.

A weigh-in was required for the top-placing cars, and as he paused on the jiggling wooden platform for a read-out, he had a surge of fear. Each race car had a minimum weight requirement; maybe Larry had made sure the car was underweight, too. But the scale registered 3,260 pounds—60 pounds to the good. Trace let out a breath.

After a victory lap with the winner's circle checkered flag (not Maurice's—it might get smudged), Trace stopped on the black-and-white checkerboard of concrete directly across from the grandstand. Handing the checkered flag to one of Maurice's spotters, he killed the engine and pulled himself out. The spotter returned the flag for the photographs, and Trace waved it at the crowd, which continued to clap.

"Ladies and gentlemen, this is Trace Bonham's first feature win! You saw it right here at Headwaters Speedway!" announced Art from the booth. Even Mel leaned out the window to clap and wave at Trace.

The driver of orange No. 27 came by with a gloved hand held out to Trace—all five fingers. Trace stepped over for a quick high five. Then No. 27's driver spun his tires—one driver's salute to another—and headed to the pits.

Trace knelt beside his yellow No. 32 for the first of several photographs. Below Maurice's flag stand, a small gate opened, and the "trophy kid" and his mom were escorted across the track toward the winner's circle. Chosen by a drawing, kids had their photos taken with winning drivers. The kids also got small trophies of their own. Trace had always thought it was a little cheesy—until now. A blond-haired boy, about five years old, came across the rutted dirt clutching his mother's hand. He looked scared and excited.

"Hey, little dude," Trace said. He peeled off his sweaty race gloves and shook hands with the kid. The boy looked wide-eyed at Trace—at his uniform, at the car.

"Ready?" said a local newspaper photographer. Beside him was a guy who wrote for *Big Dirt* magazine; he also pointed a camera.

Trace and the boy smiled for their pictures, the little guy clutching his little trophy, Trace holding his big one. The boy kept looking around—at Trace's car, at Trace. He reached out a pudgy finger to touch Trace's trophy. Trace looked at the boy's tiny trophy. "Here," he said. "You take the big one."

The little boy's eyes widened as if Trace was Santa Claus and it was Christmas morning. The trophy was almost as tall as he was. The youngish, tanned mom gave Trace a giant hug and big kiss on the cheek. Cameras flashed.

"I could get used to this," Trace said.

"Me, too, dear," she said, and gave him an extra hug.

"Whoa!" Trace replied. He looked quickly up at the announcer's booth, hoping Mel hadn't seen that.

Back in the pits, Trace got his third big hug of the night—though not a kiss—from his dad.

"Wow. Now that was driving," his father said, his voice thick with emotion. He released Trace and stepped back as if to get the full measure of his son.

"What, you got sand in your eyes?" Trace said.

"Something like that," his father said, wiping at them. He tried to speak, but his voice broke.

"Hey, Dad, it's all right."

"You're sure?" Don asked. "I should have listened to you—"

"Really. It's okay. We're good." And he hugged his father again.

"Your trophy!" his father said suddenly. "Jeez—that was your first feature win and you gave it away."

"There's plenty more hardware where that came from," Trace said.

BEAU

Talk about luck of the draw—Beau started the Mod-Four feature seventh row, inside. Even though the water truck had chugged around after the Super Stocks, the cars ahead were already kicking up dust. The haze was only going to get worse this far back. The track lights were on now, which brightened the dust like a storm of brown snow in high-beam headlamps. Under his helmet visor he wore a red bandanna tight across his nose and mouth. New helmets had built-in dust filters, but those models cost hundreds of dollars.

He caught a glimpse, on the opposite turn, of Amber's red No. 13a. She was third row, outside. That put her five cars off the leader and up high, where she could see to make a move.

Rolling two columns wide at yellow-flag speed, the twenty Mod-Fours came around bumper to bumper, wheel to wheel. The tightly bunched, orderly stream of cars approached turn 3. It was always a question of when the pole position car would pull the trigger—and bolt toward the anticipated green flag. If the lead car powered up too soon, the trailing cars usually got spread out and misaligned—which required a restart. Wait too long to put the pedal down, and the drivers behind the pole car got impatient and tried to run over the front-runners.

Tonight the lead cars held an even pace deep into turn 3.

"Come on, come on!" Beau said. It was like they were teasing the cars farther back—and the crowd as well. A ragged wave passed across the bleachers as the fans rose to their feet. With a sudden whine of engines and an explosion of dust, the lead cars surged forward. Maurice squinted a long moment, then waved the green flag furiously. Beau stamped his accelerator to the floor and went flat out with the others. A light-colored car surged past on Beau's right side—and out came the yellow flag. Somebody had jumped the gun.

As they went around again for realignment on the restart, Maurice leaned far over his white railing and waggled his yellow flag directly at silver No. 55.

"I knew it," Beau said.

Like a referee throwing a penalty flag, Maurice jerked his yellow stick at No. 55 and sent him tail back, or to the rear. Beau couldn't resist. He waggled his index finger at the black-helmeted driver, who responded with a different finger in a vertical position.

On the restart—a clean one this time—Beau cut to the outside. No. 55 soon surged on his tail. Beau cut off his line and held him back. Not that Beau was parked on the track or didn't have power. Toward the end of the qualifying heat, his engine took on a slightly different sound. A higher-pitched whine. Something inside his motor had loosened, was running more freely. The more wear inside the cylinders, the more easily the pistons moved—new, "tight" engines were way overrated—and tonight Beau's old Ford block was hitting the high notes. It had more punch, more rpm, more horsepower than ever in its lifetime.

Which was not a good sign. An engine increasing in rpm and horsepower was like a hard drive "wrapping," like the adrenaline run of a heart-shot deer. His engine was going to blow—break a piston, swallow a valve, shoot a pushrod through the head—but with any luck, not for at least twenty laps.

Streaming by on the outside, he decoyed a cluster of out-of-town Mod-Fours into the soft spot in turn 1. As they approached it, he dove low. The other cars, seeing an opening, surged into the trap—rocking and rolling through the turn like drunks staggering after one another. Silver No. 55 took the hook, too, and bounced to the high side—and almost over the edge.

"Eat dust!" Beau shouted. In his head he put the situation into textbook terms.

If Train A leaves the station at 8:40 p.m. traveling at fifty-five miles per hour, and Train B leaves the station at 8:41 traveling at fifty-six miles per hour, how long will it take Train B to catch up with Train A?

"About a hundred laps, sucker!"

At lap 12, No. 55 showed up a half-length off his right rear wheel. *Bam*—there he was—the man in black—nudging and bumping—trying to get past. By then Beau was running in fifth place. Ahead in the fine dust were patches of red—Amber Jenkins herself. Beau fought off No. 55 and tucked in tight behind Amber. She momentarily lost her line in turn 3, and Beau slipped past her. She looked at him—stunned, he could tell. But he had no time to savor the moment. Ahead, the leading Mod-Fours were a trio of fish darting through cloudy water. Through fine brown algae, suspended in hanging curtains, like in a Minnesota lake in late summer. Beau pressed after them only yards, then feet, then inches behind. He drove flat out, drove nearly blind.

By lap 15, something weird had happened. Noise receded. His engine whine, the rasp of tire-to-tire contact, the shriek of metal on metal—all sound shrank away. Cars around him swam in silence. Doorways, odd shafts of light appeared in the dust. He dove his little No. 19z at them, slipping through like a minnow between sunlit reeds. Again he found a seam, a porthole, and darted through, passing another car. He was in the Zone, that magic place that drivers—that athletes in general—live for.

"Yeah, baby!" Beau called to his car. "Stay with me!" Four laps to go. His engine sounded like a blender punched up beyond Puree. Some other racer was going to protest Beau's engine for sure—which made him laugh out loud. "Tear it down, take a look," he shouted, weaving behind the leaders, riding their tails, driving hard into the corners. "But gimme the cash right now."

He poised himself to make a run at the leader, blue No. 47. Three laps to go.

AMBER

When Beau passed her, she couldn't believe it. Her first instinct was to run him off the road—that or clap. But he came by too fast for her to pinch his line, and with clapping there was the small problem of driving with no hands. She settled for good old anger. She hated being passed by anyone, even Beau. Especially Beau.

Pushing No. 13a to the limit, she inched up on him—until her front left tire caught a rut. Not a serious rut, but enough to wobble her and take away her straight-line thrust. Suddenly she was five car lengths back. Right behind her appeared silver No. 55.

"You again," she muttered.

He tried to pass high. She blocked him. He tried low. She cut him off on the inside. His car had more punch than hers (he was probably an engine cheat), but she managed to fend him off and hold on to third place as the laps counted down.

When she knew she could not catch Beau or the blue No. 47, she concentrated on staying solidly in third place. Silver No. 55 wanted third badly—rocked her from behind, then pretended to dive left. She didn't take the bait and stayed straight on. He remained locked up behind her, pounding his steering wheel in a rage.

Which was when it happened.

Looking frontward into turn 1, where she should have

been paying attention (not obsessing on No. 55), Amber saw the full underside of a car: bottom panels, driveshaft, chassis, four tires. None of it was anywhere near the ground. A second car skidded sideways through the dense brown dust, its axle plowing dirt, its right front tire gone. The flying car, which must have clipped No. 47, hung in the air. No numbers, no names, just the oddly clean underside of a Mod-Four race car. It came down pink and black.

"Beau!" she shouted. He flipped pink over black, pink over black. His arms began to flap. On the second flip, his roof collapsed and his roll cage split open like a parakeet cage thrown to the ground.

The bird came out of the cage. Beau shot through the broken pipes of his roll cage, shoulder harness flapping behind. One of the shoulder harness bolts must have broken—or its washer and nut pulled through the floor. Beau ended up sitting unbelted in the dirt beside his car—which looked like a display of aluminum lawn chairs crushed by a forklift.

Amber had already hit the skids, and now she cranked her wheel to the right. She pitched her car into a long four-wheel, sideways drift. Time slowed from seconds to minutes to hours to days—then to seasonal time, glacial time. It was all a question of whether she could stop soon enough to protect Beau from oncoming traffic—or slide into him and crush him against his wrecked No. 19z.

The No. 55 car slid by down low and in the clear, but Amber took hits from other cars—rocking her side to side, pivoting her car wildly—still, she held her slide. Beau's white helmet wobbled groggily as Amber drifted closer. Then his visor steadied, face out, as the red side of Amber's No. 13a slid toward him. He held out his hands palms up—as if that would do any good. Amber took another hard shot, a crashing blow to her right front side, which drove her car's left front nose into Beau's junk heap—and created for him a little triangle, a slash of open dirt, a safe place.

She was stopped. Noise and dust sucked away as if vacuumed by a giant hose. Amber leaned out her window and looked down at Beau. "You okay?"

"Whaa . . . happened?" he said, raising his visor.

"Everything!" Amber said, pulling herself rapidly through her side window. There was a strong gasoline smell. "Anything broken?"

Beau's right hand fell onto a piece of broken roll cage pipe. He held it up. "Like my whole car?" Tires pointed in different directions, the rims were bent, the chassis wrenched, the roof crushed.

"Forget about your car. It's toast."

At that point a four-wheeler driven by Johnny Walters skidded to a stop, followed closely by an ambulance. The other race cars were halted under Maurice's red flag.

"Move away from the cars if you can," Johnny called. With a fire extinguisher he blew white foam on Beau's smoking engine.

"I'm okay!" Beau said, standing up. With Beau leaning

on Amber, his arm over her shoulders, her arm tight around his waist, they walked away. Stepped into the clear.

In the stands, the crowd rose to their feet and clapped and cheered.

Beau looked across the infield. "Jeez, I hope my mom isn't here."

=== *JOHNNY*

Johnny helped get Beau's car on the wrecker's hook, then he and his spotters made sure the track was clear of debris. After the Mod-Four restart, he drove down pit row to check on Beau Kim. Silver No. 55 came by in the lead on the final laps, but Johnny's focus was on the Mod-Four kids.

Beau sat on the one tire of No. 192 that wasn't flat. He was surrounded by his crew and Amber's as well. His Mod-Four—totaled and then some—lay behind them. The car, with its broken chassis pipes sticking up in all directions, looked like it had been hit by a roadside bomb.

"You're sure you're okay?" Johnny said.

Beau nodded. "The ambulance guys looked me over. I'm fine."

"He's a wrestler," one of Beau's crew said. "He's used to getting his bell rung."

"And pinned," said another skinny kid.

"I was *not* pinned out there," Beau said. "Was I?" He looked at Amber.

"No, not pinned. Just relaxing beside your car in the middle of the track."

"That was quite a maneuver," Johnny said to Amber.

She shrugged.

Beau's eyes stayed on her.

"Not every driver would even have tried it," Johnny added.

"No big deal," Amber said. "I just hate seeing roadkill. Things squashed on the highway?" She shuddered. "Ish. Turtles are the worst."

"Hey, I was no turtle out there tonight," Beau said.

"That's true," Amber said. "I'd protest your engine, but there's nothing left."

"We've got a spare Ford block he can borrow," Amber's brother Joe said. "Needs a new head. Other than that, it's good to go."

Beau looked at his flattened car. "I'd sorta need something to hang it in."

"Maybe we can get that figured out," Johnny said. "I know some guys who know some guys."

Beau allowed himself part of a smile.

Across the track, silver No. 55 paused on the scales, then pulled into the winner's circle for photographs. The driver, a surprisingly small guy, got out and knelt with the checkered flag and the trophy kid. Cameras flashed.

"There's no justice," Dweeb muttered.

Amber's brothers had way worse things to say.

"Racing is not one night, it's a career," Johnny said to the two young drivers and their crews. "Remember that, all right?"

They nodded but kept grumbling.

"And, yes, what goes around, comes around," Johnny said. "Someday that guy will get his."

After a quick victory lap, silver No. 55 pulled into the pits.

"Don't look at him," Amber said, pretending to be busy with her helmet.

"Him?" Dweeb said. "Him?"

They looked up. Helmet off, the driver of silver No. 55 slowed by Amber and Beau. Behind the wheel was a girl, nineteen, maybe twenty, with chopped black hair and a nose ring.

"Whoa!" Guitar Hero breathed.

"No way," Johnny murmured. He looked at his clipboard.

"You all right?" the driver called to Beau.

"Yeah," Beau said. "Sort of."

The black-haired girl turned to Amber. "Sweet move out there."

"As if you care," Amber said.

"Not really," the girl said. "I just like to win." She spun her tires as she departed.

"Listen, you—" Amber began, but Guitar Hero drowned her out.

"Who *was* that chick?"

Johnny looked up from his clipboard. "I checked her car in, and I heard the name Terry. But she signed in as Terri Huckabee. She had a cap on. I didn't notice she was a girl."

Amber's brothers immediately hooted and laughed at Johnny.

Amber was not amused. "Terri, huh? I'll tear her a new one next time I see her," she growled.

"I'm sure you will," Johnny said as he fired up his four-wheeler to escape any more abuse from Amber's brothers. He drove on with a smile. Racing was in good hands. The future was here tonight, and he liked everything about it.

Except for the weather.

Thunder pounded only a few miles to the west. Horizontal lightning stitched the dark wall of the oncoming front. In the pits came louder thunder—the Late Model class rumbling onto the track.

"Ladies and gentlemen," Art Lempola announced. "We've got weather coming in, so we're going to get started just as quick as we can. But due to a great crowd tonight, plus all the special guest drivers from across Minnesota, Johnny Walters himself is bumping up the purse to one thousand dollars to win."

The crowd stamped their feet wildly.

"I'm bumping the purse?" Johnny asked as the crowd continued to stamp the wooden bleachers.

"Is that all right, Dad?" Melody's voice came in his

headset as if she were reading his mind. "I think it will get some of those big teams back here to race again this summer."

Johnny paused. "Hey, baby, it's only money."

"I'm not in favor of this," Maurice said into Johnny's headset. "It'll just make the locals more aggressive and cause more restarts."

"Let's have fun, Maurice," Johnny said, with a glance at the sky. "But get 'em going ASAP."

TUDY

Finally there were no more customers in line at the Waggin. Everyone was back in the stands for the last race of the loudest cars. She could never remember what the bigger cars were called, and she didn't really care. "It's over a hundred degrees!" she said, pointing to the little thermometer on the wall.

"It's probably two hundred over here," her mother said from the fry bread cooker. Her face gleamed with sweat. Leonard seemed unbothered by the heat, though he had been icing his head.

"Good time for a break," Ritchie called. His face was shiny and redder than a September tomato. "Why don't you get some fresh air before the last rush? I'll stay here."

"Go check the weather," Winona said to Tudy. "I keep thinking I hear thunder, but maybe it's the cars."

Tudy and Leonard stepped down from the wagon.

"Don't be gone long," Ritchie called after her. "We got more buns to slice." Tudy muttered something under her breath, then jerked her head for Leonard to follow. In the darker parking lot, they walked along in silence.

"Your folks are nice," Leonard ventured.

Tudy shrugged. "I hate working the wagon."

"Nobody makes fry bread like your mom," Leonard said. They walked on in silence. His hand brushed hers—and suddenly they were holding hands. They walked the length of one whole row of cars.

"How come you stay up on the rez?" Tudy asked suddenly. "It's scary up there."

Leonard shrugged. "Everybody knows me there," he said. "And I know the rez. I'd miss the lake. The gym."

"You could come down here and go to school—and probably be on the basketball team's starting five."

Leonard was silent.

"Anyway, you should think about it."

"I will," he said.

A sudden breath of cool breeze washed over them. "Oh, wow!" Tudy said. "That feels so good!" She raised her arms high and turned in a slow circle. She let the fresh air bathe her. She wished it could touch all of her skin, every part of her body. She kept turning in a circle.

Leonard watched her. "You go to powwows?"

"Sometimes," she said, lowering her arms.

Leonard was silent. "I go, but I don't dance."

"Why not?"

"I don't know. I can't explain it."

"Me neither," Tudy said. She stopped turning, and they walked on. At the end of the row, they started down another one, closer to the trees, where there was less light from the speedway. "Look!" Tudy whispered. In a pickup, two teenagers were making out like crazy. They couldn't have cared less about the races.

She and Leonard giggled and sneaked past undetected.

"You could be a fancy dancer," Leonard said. "I like how they turn in circles. Like eagles flying. You would be great."

"I'd feel dumb, dancing," Tudy said abruptly.

"Why?" Leonard said.

Tudy was silent. Thunder went *ba-boom!* Under the dusty halo of the speedway lights, engines rumbled as the big cars surged onto the track for the last race. "I don't know. I just don't think it's for me."

"I know what you mean," Leonard said.

They walked on, watching the sky, holding hands tightly.

Back at the wagon, Winona was waiting for them. She checked her watch. "Where have you *been?*"

"Walking," Tudy said, with a sideways glance at Leonard. "You asked us to check the weather, so we did. We went where we could see the sky."

"And?" her mother said with annoyance.

"It's going to rain in about fifteen minutes," Leonard said softly.

SONNY

Done for the night, Sonny headed to the grandstand to watch the Late Model feature. But first he stopped at the Waggin for a sandwich.

Leonard ducked his head below the counter, but too late.

"Hey, Leonard, how's the headache?" Sonny said.

"Not all that good," Leonard said.

"I'm sure," Sonny said with a glance to Ritchie and Winona. They tried not to smile. Ritchie's face was heated up as red as Santa Claus.

"Heard you broke down," Ritchie said.

Leonard winced.

"Happens," Sonny said cheerfully, and pumped barbecue sauce onto his sandwich. "Me and Leonard will go through the engine this week."

"We will?" Leonard said.

"If we want to race next Saturday night, we will," Sonny added.

"Okay," Leonard said quickly.

Sonny headed into the stands in time to see the Late

Models getting lined up. The infield spotters, wearing bright safety vests and headphones, leaned close and pointed flags at the slowly circling cars; they moved this driver up a slot and that driver back one. It always took several laps to get everybody in the correct position. At low rpm, the big V-8 engines threw down a combined rumble that hummed in the fillings of his teeth. These motors came from professional speed shops. They cost more than his whole car—more than his whole house up on the reservation. He wasn't sure where his next engine was going to come from—maybe Ozzie's salvage yard had a junker—but he would worry about that tomorrow.

Finally, when every driver knew his spot, Art Lempola announced, "And now, in a salute to all you race fans—"

The noise from the crowd drowned him out. As one, the fans rose to their feet to stamp and cheer as the Late Models came by the grandstand slow, four wide, and tight together. The actual race would start in a column two cars wide, but this was a traditional display for the fans before every big race.

The drivers waved gloved hands to the crowd. The cheering got louder. Sonny himself, who had raced for many years, got goose bumps on his arms. He looked around at the people—Native and white, men and women, young and old all bunched together. Everybody was the same at the racetrack. They were all focused on the cars. Everybody had his or her favorite driver.

Sonny was betting on the best local driver, John Sitz

and his yellow No. 29. Cal Hopkins had drawn the fif-
teenth inside slot.

"They'll box Cal in—he'll never catch up," someone
said to Sonny.

"Don't bet on it," Sonny replied easily to an overweight white guy whom he didn't know. But the man knew
Sonny.

"Sorry you broke down tonight, Sonny. We was rooting
for you," the man's wife said.

"Thanks," Sonny said, and shook hands with them
both.

"You should move up anyway, Sonny," her husband
said. "We been watching you for years. You should be driving a Late Model, even a sprint car."

Sonny smiled and shrugged. "Too expensive for my
blood."

"The casino's got money—they could afford to sponsor you," the man persisted.

"Not all Indians like casinos," Sonny said, his smile
slipping just a bit.

The guy's wife leaned over. "Sonny, could you sign my
cap?"

"Sure." Several kids saw Sonny and hurried over to get
their T-shirts signed. Then Maurice threw the green flag,
and the Late Models surged past the grandstand. The race
was on.

The pack of Late Models came cleanly out of turn 1—
always dicey—and turn 2 as well. With their long front

hoods, they were like greyhounds, necks outstretched and flying. By the second lap, the cars had started to string out nicely. Nothing worse than a lot of restarts early in a race—especially tonight. Cooler air washed across the grandstand; lighting flickered just beyond the west tree line.

Cal Hopkins drove steady and smart. He was in no hurry. Ahead, the local favorite, John Sitz, picked up two places in his yellow No. 29; the crowd thundered their approval—as did actual thunder. A heavy *ta-boom!* rocked the grandstand. A few droplets of rain fell, but all eyes returned to the race.

By lap 15 of the thirty-lap feature, Cal Hopkins was running tenth. He was fearless. He went deep in the turns at full power and inches from—or touching tin with—the car in front. The local drivers ran strongly as well. Matt Darby challenged Hopkins on the straightaway, but in the turns Darby's left front tire bobbed freely; there was light and dust underneath it.

"That's not what you want," Sonny murmured. Cornering on three tires looked good in photos, but the fastest cars—like those of Hopkins and Sitz—had better centers of gravity, and that kept all four wheels on the ground.

Gradually Hopkins passed Darby and, one by one, three more local cars. The crowd rose to their feet. Diehard fans began to help their drivers along—pointing at them as they came by, then flinging their hands onward, down the track, as if to give their favorite cars more horse-power, more speed.

Rain spattered harder now, cutting the dust. The dirt suddenly had more bite, more traction. Cars with the best setups, mostly from out of town, moved up. They had the right suspension, the right compression on their shock absorbers, the right stagger on their wheels, the right camber on their tires. Local drivers, without the latest and most expensive technology, fell back—except for yellow No. 29.

As the rain came quicker and colder, John Sitz and Cal Hopkins battled for real. Hopkins had more power, but Sitz was more consistent in the turns. Sitz was first, Hopkins second—and vice versa—back and forth. The crowd danced and cheered. A downright cold wind began to blow; rain angled sideways to wet the fans' faces, but they shrugged it off. At most they removed their glasses and jerked down their cap brims or hoods. Their faces trickled dusty water like mascara running on men and women alike. Nobody cared about getting wet—not with four laps to go.

Sonny saw Maurice glance up to the announcer's booth, but there was no way Mel and Johnny would stop this race now. The track itself was still sucking up the moisture like a brown sponge. There was no danger of spinouts—at least for the moment. Cold, fresh air quickened the engines, too. Sonny didn't have a stopwatch, but he knew that lap speeds had never been faster. He could feel himself in the cockpit. He knew the dirt, the ruts, the soft spots, the sweet lines.

"Come on, John!" he murmured.

Under the white flag and white rain—it was that heavy—Sitz and Hopkins rocked and bumped each other through turn 3. The crowd noise reached a crescendo— like during the last round of a heavyweight boxing match when the fighters know the match is even and go for broke.

Sitz made his move on the last turn. Running on the outside a quarter-length off Hopkins's nose, he gambled on the apex of the turn. He tried to get that tiny extra bit of sling out of the corner. But his rear end slithered, came loose, and his nose hooked downward into the side of Hopkins's green No. 42. Both cars lost their grip on the wet, slick clay. As if in slow motion, the green and yellow Late Models swapped ends.

Like two colored pinwheels spinning side by side, like two polka dancers twirling, the cars turned 360s straight down the track and underneath Maurice's checkered flag.

By the angle of his turning, the green nose of Cal Hopkins's car passed first—and won the checkered. But that was the least of anyone's concern. Hopkins kept spinning all the way into the infield, with Sitz bearing down hard. Somehow Sitz managed to get control of his car—and missed the sitting duck Hopkins by a short car length. The cars suddenly sat silent, parked perfectly side by side in the rain.

The crowd, which had sucked in their breath and gone silent, let out a roar that probably was heard in town, five miles away.

MEL

After the Late Model feature, Mel hurried across the wet track and the infield with many of the fans. People liked to step onto the track. They liked to feel the dirt under their feet—even if it was muddy and slick. They liked to talk to the drivers, look at the cars. *Snak-boom!* went the lightning and thunder. Shielding her face, she glanced up at the osprey nest, silent above the humming lights. Someday lightning was going to hit that nest, but please not tonight, she thought.

"Mel!" Patrick called. He hurried over. He was smiling, wet, and relaxed in his jeans and cowboy boots; he didn't look at all like a choir geek.

"What a race!" he said. "Did you see the finish?"

"No, I wasn't watching," Mel said—then felt bad. She had to work on not being so sarcastic.

"Anyway," Patrick said with a shrug.

"It was a great race, no doubt about it!" Mel said. "You want to meet Cal Hopkins?"

"Really?" Patrick said.

"Sure. Let's go," Mel said. Braving the rain, they joined

the throngs heading toward the Late Model area. Ahead, Cal's crew had their trailer lit up and waiting, its drop-leaf counter piled high with souvenir T-shirts and sweatshirts and caps, a rain tarp overhead. Cal himself, sweaty and dusty, sat under a big umbrella at a small table, signing autographs.

"Mel, Patrick!" Trace called from the side.

They turned. Trace, still in his racing suit, his hair wet, angled through the crowd.

"Hey, great race!" Patrick said, and threw a hug on Trace. Trace hugged him back. Mel stared.

"You two are, like, friends?" she asked.

"Hey, I should have given that trophy to him," Trace said to Mel, with a nod to Patrick.

"I'm confused," Mel said.

"It's a long story," Trace said. "Come on, let's get in line. I want to get an autograph."

"Speaking of new friends," Mel said, "how about that mom in the winner's circle?"

"Mom? What mom?" Trace said, biting his lip.

"Yeah, right," Mel answered.

They waited with the others, hunched against the rain, which had lightened just a bit. They talked excitedly. Trace told the story of Butt Crack Larry. Patrick talked about Beau Kim's crash, which they agreed was certain to make the sports section of the local paper.

"Dad's going to help him get another car put together," Mel said.

"How nice," Trace said flatly.

Mel looked sideways at him. "Hey, Beau could have been killed."

"Sorry. You're right," Trace said. "It's just that Kim's not my favorite dude, if you know what I mean."

"That V-8 versus import thing?" Mel said.

"No. We just don't like each other."

"Maybe you two should, like, be adults and talk that through," Mel said. "Though that doesn't seem to be your strong suit."

"Yeah, sorry," Trace said. He knew what she was referring to.

"My dad's going to want to talk to you about the fight," she said.

"I figured that," Trace said, glancing around.

"It will probably cost you. Rules are rules," Mel said.

"Did I ask for a break?" Trace asked sharply, an edge of anger in his voice.

"No, you didn't," Mel said quickly.

"Hey, hey—let's look at T-shirts," Patrick said to lighten the mood.

"As if I can afford one," Trace grumbled. Mel laughed and tugged his arm.

Patrick bought a bright T-shirt with Cal's No. 42 car in fluorescent green bursting through orange flames on a black cotton background.

"*Now* you can hang with me at school," Trace said.

Soon they were in front of Cal's table.

"Mr. Hopkins?" Mel said shyly. She put out her hand. "I'm Mel—Melody—Walters."

His gray-blue eyes lit up. "Well. I knew you were smart, and I should have known you'd be pretty." He stood up and shook her hand.

She laughed and felt herself turn pink; luckily the lights in the pit area were not that bright. "I'm wondering if you could sign my program."

"My pleasure," he said. "In fact, why don't you and your dad come around later? I've got a few stories about Johnny that I could tell."

"For sure! And these are my friends, Patrick and Trace," she said quickly.

"They can come, too," Cal said.

"Could you sign my T-shirt?" Patrick said.

Cal took care of it.

"And my racing suit?" Trace said, stepping forward.

Cal squinted at Trace. "What class you run in, son?"

"Just Street Stock," Trace said.

"Never say 'just,' " Cal said, leaning close to write on Trace's uniform, chest area, left side. "I'd like to know who was driving that yellow No. 32 Street Stock. That guy's got a future."

There was silence—then Mel burst out laughing. "You're looking at him," she said. "Trace Bonham."

Cal cocked his head. He took a long look at Trace, then lowered his voice. "You got something else to write on, Trace?"

"Ah, not really," Trace stammered.

"Here's my program," Mel said quickly.

Cal took it and wrote down a phone number. "This is my shop. I want you to call me next week. Wednesday would be good."

Trace's Adam's apple bounced in his throat like he was about to spit up a golf ball. "Wow! Sure! Wednesday!"

"There's a new Super Stock ride opening up," Cal said. "Full sponsor, a real team. I hear that they're looking for a young driver. I think you should try out."

Trace had no words.

"Come on, Trace," Mel said, tugging his arm, "you can talk to Cal later."

Cal turned to the next fans waiting in line. "Hi there," he said. "Thanks for coming out to Headwaters."

As they walked away, Trace glanced back at Cal Hopkins's trailer. "I can't believe it," he breathed.

"You owe me!" Mel said, walking between the two boys.

"No kidding," Trace said. He turned and stared at her for a long moment.

"You, too," Mel said, turning to Patrick.

"I do?" Patrick said, sticking close on her other side.

"I should have fired you for almost breaking that Pure Stock guy's neck!"

They walked on. Up ahead they saw Sonny Down Wind with his own crowd of admirers, including Tudy Thompson-Gurneau. She was standing close to a tall kid with a long black ponytail.

"That's that basketball dude, Leonard, from the rez," Trace said. "He averages like thirty points. He's something else—I've seen him play."

"Is Ritchie going to bring the Waggin over to the pits tonight?" Mel called to Tudy.

She didn't hear. She was too busy leaning on Leonard, who had slipped an arm around her waist.

"I think that's a yes," Trace said. "He always does. Man, am I hungry."

Just beyond Tudy and Sonny's group, Beau Kim was talking to an out-of-town Mod-Four team. Mel and the two boys headed his way.

"It's tough to wreck like that," the crew chief said to Beau. A helper nodded.

"I guess my racing career is pretty much over," Beau said, shoulders slumped, "unless I can patch together a ride. You know, from stuff other people don't need."

"That can work," the older man said. "Is there any-thing in particular you could use?"

"Maybe a head for a Ford 2300 block," Beau said quickly. His eyes flickered to Amber, who waited nearby; he winked.

"Hmmmm. You know, I think we have one in the trailer," the crew guy said. "Let me look."

Amber waved to Mel.

"Hey," Trace said to Beau.

Beau nodded. "Congrats."

"Thanks. Tough night for you," Trace said.

"Yeah, but I'll be back," Beau said. He turned back to

his work as the man produced a Ford head, valves intact, for his inspection.

"Really, I couldn't," Beau said. "It's too much."

"No. I want you to take it," the man said. "Sometimes a guy needs a little help."

"Well, thanks," Beau said. He paused, then asked, "You wouldn't have a carburetor for this lying around?"

Mel, Trace, and Patrick walked on. "I've got to learn how he does that," Trace said, looking back at Beau.

"Speaking of learning stuff, you said you wished you could sing," Patrick said.

"I did?" Trace said, with a glance to Mel.

"Yes, you did," Patrick said quickly.

"Okay, okay, I did," Trace said. "So?"

"So you should join choir."

"Me? In choir?" Trace asked. He stopped walking.

"Why not?" Patrick said. "It's where all the pretty girls are."

"Whoa," Trace said, pausing to let that thought turn through his brain. "It's true." He turned to look at Mel.

"Join choir—or not," Patrick said, realizing his stupidity.

"Come on!" Trace called, pulling Melody's arm, "let's find a dry spot."

"Yeah, my boots are wrecked," Patrick said.

"They needed to get wrecked," Trace said. "Muddy and all scuffed up. *Now* you can wear them to school."

The nearest dry place was in Cal Hopkins's big car

trailer. A whole bunch of people crowded in, including Johnny on his ATV, Beau and Amber, Tudy and her Leonard, Sonny, George and Maurice, Mel and Patrick and Trace—plus a handful of fans who thought they had died and gone to race car heaven.

"Wow," Trace said, looking around.

"And then some," Mel said. The tall, brightly lit trailer had a black-and-white checkerboard floor that was cleaner—at least for the moment—than most people's kitchen floors. A spare chassis hung from the ceiling. Rear ends and axles were clamped on the upper side walls. Aluminum racks and bins of spare parts lined the lower walls. In the front of the trailer was a wide rack of fresh tires on rims; to the right was a car-ready engine sealed in plastic, along with curving exhaust headers. Beside the engine was some kind of dyno with blinking red digital readouts. Powering everything, a generator hummed somewhere outside.

"Don't worry about the floor," Cal said. "Johnny's people will mop it later."

People laughed and crowded inside. Sonny, Leonard, and Tudy squeezed in the rear just out of the rain. Cal perched on the tire rack so he could see everyone. Johnny sat on his ATV beside him.

"Well, here we are. Might as well make the best of it until the rain stops," Cal said.

"Speech," somebody called out.

"All right, why not?" Cal said. "First, I'd like to thank

Mel—Melody Walters—for getting me over here tonight. This track has a lot of potential—and a great owner. With a great daughter. Come on up here, Mel."

There was clapping inside the long trailer.

When Mel was situated next to her dad, Cal's face turned serious. "Some of you younger fans might not know what a great driver Johnny Walters was," he said. "You know him as a man on an ATV and in his wheelchair. I knew him as black No. 14a, a sprint car driver who could take you to school any night of the week."

The crowd quieted. Johnny shrugged. Mel draped an arm around her father's shoulders.

"Let me tell you about his career," Cal said. He went through the wins, the highlights, the different racetracks, all the stories. The rain continued. Then Cal paused and lowered his voice. "Which brings me to that night down in Knoxville."

The trailer went totally silent but for the soft, wet thrashing on the roof. "I was there, running about eighth behind Johnny," Cal began. "Johnny was in fourth, ready to make a move. I was a young gun myself, then," Cal said. "I thought I was bulletproof. To me, Johnny was the mark, the man to beat."

The rain, and the story, continued. Damp clothes and body heat slowly filled the trailer with humidity, with the mingled scents of perfume, motor oil, tobacco, sweat, leather, chain saw—and Ritchie's barbecue sauce on people's breath.

"I thought I had a good line up high. I made a move. For some reason I had lots of power that night. Nobody could touch me on the straightaway—except Johnny, maybe."

No one stirred.

"He wasn't about to be passed high and came up to pinch me off. Or something like that. Maybe he didn't even see me. Anyway, suddenly there he was right in front of me."

Mel held her breath.

"I thought I'd bump him—just a little tap. That was all. I just wanted to send Johnny a message that I was there. That I was somebody to reckon with."

Johnny dropped his chin. Mel held on to him tighter.

"I did, and suddenly Johnny's all loose and sideways. Then, well, then everything went to hell."

Mel closed her eyes. For the first time she could really see it. She understood how racing—and life itself—turned on a split second here, an inch there.

"I remember running over Johnny," Cal said, his voice almost at a whisper. "Then another car ran over me. After that, well, it was pretty much lights out until the ambulance guys came. But when I came to, I knew what I'd done," Cal said. "That night has stayed with me every day of my life. People have wondered, and I'll tell you right here. That accident was why I dropped down to Late Models and Super Stocks," he finished. "I was never quite right in a sprint car again."

Johnny looked up. "I never thought it was your fault," he said softly. "I never blamed you. I remember getting bumped on the left side. You were on my right. There was bumping all over. We all thought we were bulletproof that night."

Cal stared.

"We just all got wrapped up in each other, and we wrecked. That's the way I see it," Johnny said.

"Some of us got by easier than others," Cal said, his voice threatening to break.

"True," Johnny replied. "But am I complaining?" He looked around the trailer. "The answer is—yes!"

Everybody laughed, with relief in their voices.

"No, that's not true," Johnny said. "I've got spaghetti noodles for legs, I own a one-horse speedway—but I have a great crew." He pointed to George and Maurice, Patrick and the others.

People clapped.

"And a really great daughter!" Johnny finished.

"You're right about that," Cal said. Trace and Patrick clapped, as did the crowd, and Mel managed a smile.

Cal looked straight at her. "One more thing. I have to ask—Mel, what do you want to do with your life?"

"Like, get through my senior year?" Mel shot back.

"First things first," Cal said, "that's good. But I want you to know, Mel, that there are jobs out there in racing. I know a lot of speedways that are dying for want of a good chief operations officer—somebody to really run the show."

"I could do that," Mel said.

"No doubt," Cal answered. Just then a shiny, wet pickup and silver trailer pulled up. It was Ritchie and Winona with the Waggin.

Ritchie poked his head out the pickup's window. "Last call!"

Though the rain still fell, Cal's trailer emptied in a hurry. Sonny lingered; Mel nudged her father.

"Hey, Sonny, come up and meet Cal," Johnny said.

Later, as Mel was locking the main gate to the empty speedway, she turned to look back. The rain had washed everything clean. The wooden bleachers, the sponsors' signs, the light poles, the mesh fence, even the concrete-block toilets—all gleamed wet and like new. The speedway looked like a child's village made of snap-together plastic blocks. "All wrapped up in each other," her father had said of the race cars. For some reason, that phrase explained a lot of things.

Above the infield, the ospreys were quiet. She imagined the chicks, warm and cozy and dry under the parents' wings. Maybe the speedway was her nest. Maybe everybody had a nest, and the racetrack was hers.

At the stop sign by the highway, with her father driving, they paused. "What did Sonny and Cal talk about?" she said suddenly. "You guys were in the trailer for a long time."

"Man talk," Johnny said with a smile.

"Yeah, yeah," Mel said.

"Actually, I told Sonny about some local sponsorship opportunities. If anybody deserves a good ride, it's him."

"Let me guess. He said he'd 'think about it,' right?" Mel said.

Johnny smiled. "That's our Sonny."

Mel's phone vibrated. It was Trace.

"What?"

"Is it Wednesday yet?"

"No." Mel checked her watch. "But it is Sunday. Go to bed."

"Has your dad said anything about my fight?"

"Not yet, but he will."

Trace let out a long breath.

"Don't worry about it, okay?"

"Okay," Trace said, and Mel folded shut her phone.

Her father looked over.

"Trace," she said.

"Big night for that boy," Johnny said. "Which reminds me—he and I have to talk. But tomorrow," he said, his voice softening.

She leaned against him. "Big night for all of us," Mel murmured.

Her dad put his arm around her, and she let her eyes drift shut. As the truck rolled home, she tried to imagine what it was like to be one of those osprey chicks—what it felt like the first time they spread their wings, caught the air, and flew.

That was what she would do—fly away from here someday. But not for a while. Not this summer or the next. One day at a time, that was the way to go. Today was Sunday, which meant there were only six more days until racing.

Go Fish!

GOFISH

WILL WEAVER

What did you want to be when you grew up?
Not a clue. (What fun would being a clue be?)

When did you realize you wanted to be a writer?
I grew up on a farm, and did not come from a family of writers, so I was really old—like twenty-five—before I realized that I wanted to write seriously.

What's your first childhood memory?
My grandfather's big, rough, loving hands.

What's your most embarrassing childhood memory?
Going to a costume party in seventh grade that was NOT a costume party.

What's your favorite childhood memory?
Summers, walking for miles in the countryside just exploring.

As a young person, who did you look up to most?
The road grader guy. He was cool and had a great big machine to drive.

What was your worst subject in school?
Math.

What was your best subject in school?
History and English.

What was your first job?
On the farm, it was hauling firewood and collecting eggs from the coop.

How did you celebrate publishing your first book?
By almost dying. My wife and I took a short canoe trip before my book tour began; we got caught in a storm and almost capsized. Very scary.

Where you do write your books?
I have a corner library office in my house that looks out on trees, and beyond them, glints of the Mississippi River—which is clear, clean, and narrow where I live in northern Minnesota.

Where do you find inspiration for your writing?
In moment and memories that will not go out of my head. . . . They keep saying, "Remember me?"

Which of your characters is most like you?
The kid, Paul, in *Full Service*, whose first summer job was at a gas station.

When you finish a book, who reads it first?
My editor at the book publishing company. An editor is like a teacher; he or she reads the rough draft and helps me make it the best I can.

Are you a morning person or a night owl?
It's 6:30 AM as I'm writing this.

What's your idea of the best meal ever?
Fresh fish from the river, wild rice, homemade bread, and apple pie.

Which do you like better: cats or dogs?
Dogs.

What do you value most in your friends?
Their acceptance of my moods. Sometimes I just like to be around friends even though my thoughts are elsewhere—like on some fiction I'm writing.

Where do you go for peace and quiet?
My canoe on the river.

What makes you laugh out loud?
People who can laugh at themselves. It's fun to laugh with someone who tells you something stupid they just did. We've all been there.

What's your favorite song?
This varies according to my mood. . . . One day I might like loud rock, another day cool jazz.

Who is your favorite fictional character?
Ebenezer Scrooge.

What are you most afraid of?
Failure not of my imagination, but of being able to write good sentences.

What time of the year do you like best?
Autumn. October in Minnesota is the best.

What is your favorite TV show?
Not a big TV watcher.

If you were stranded on a desert island, who would you want for company?
My wife.

If you could travel in time, where would you go?
Paris, May, 1913, to the opera house where Stravinsky debuted "The Rite of Spring." This musical composition was so radical for the time, it causes riots in the streets. Talk about the power of art!

What's the best advice you have ever received about writing?
"It doesn't have to be perfect, but it does have to be done (finished, that is)."

What do you want readers to remember about your books?
That the book moved them—that in some small way it changed a part of their life.

What would you do if you ever stopped writing?
I'd be a sad guy. One who had given up on life . . .

What do you like best about yourself?
I'm in good physical shape.

What is your worst habit?
Being impatient with other people.

What do you consider to be your greatest accomplishment?
Being a good father. After that, publishing my first novel.

Where in the world do you feel most at home?
In the woods, hunting deer.

What do you wish you could do better?
Play the piano.

What would your readers be most surprised to learn about you?
I'm an athlete, I hunt and fish, I have a stock car—but I also love playing the piano.

*K*eep reading for an excerpt from
Will Weaver's **Super Stock Rookie**,
available soon in hardcover from Farrar, Straus and Giroux.

EXCERPT

Trace Bonham's phone beeped in his hand. NERVOUS YET? The text message was from Patrick, who was riding with Mel in her car.

NOT YET, Trace keyed back.

Trace and his dad, Don Bonham, rolled west on U.S. Highway 2 at seventy-plus. Right behind were Mel and friends in her white Toyota. Following Mel was Tyler, Trace's pit man, alone in his Chevy pickup. Their destination: Trace's Super Stock tryout at Rivers Speedway in Grand Forks, North Dakota. On both sides of the highway, flat fields shimmered in the July heat.

His phone beeped again. HOW ABOUT NOW?

"I wish you'd put that damn phone away and get your mind right for racing!" Trace's dad said sharply. His dark brown eyes threw a glare in his son's direction.

"It's not like you don't get a few calls from Linda," Trace shot back. Linda was his father's girlfriend; Trace's mother lived in Wisconsin.

"True," his dad said. "But I also take care of business. I'm just saying that you don't get a chance like this every day. You have to be ready."

"Like I don't know that?" Trace answered. This Super Stock tryout was a huge deal to his dad. He had been obsessing on it ever since Cal Hopkins, the Late Model points leader and former sprint car driver, had seen Trace win at Headwaters Speedway earlier in the month and invited him to the tryout. Obsessing on that and Linda, a nurse in Detroit Lakes whom Trace had never met.

"For a young driver like you, this is a potentially career-making opportunity—but you have to *want* it," his dad said.

"I want it, all right?" Trace said, sudden anger in his voice.

His father fell silent.

HOW ABOUT NOW? read the text message, this time from Mel's phone.

Trace glanced over his shoulder. Mel—Melody Walters—seventeen, who managed Headwaters Speedway for her dad, was behind the wheel; she smiled and waved with both hands. She wore sunglasses and her usual World of Outlaws cap. Her car appeared to be empty. Mel put her hands behind her head like she was bored with driving, and looked off across the fields. As if on automatic pilot, her Toyota continued straight down the highway.

CUTE, Trace keyed.

A few seconds later, Patrick Fletcher and the other kids in Mel's car popped up and Mel grabbed back the steering wheel. They all laughed like fools, waving and making faces and obscene gestures at Trace like a carload of patients escaped from the nuthouse. Cute, but annoying. Patrick—whose "gofer" duties at Headwaters included singing the national anthem—got to ride with Mel, while Trace was stuck for two hours with his dad in their big Chevy Tahoe.

"I wish we could have kept this whole thing more under wraps," his father said, glancing into the rearview mirror.

Trace faked a yawn, certain to annoy his dad, and tipped back his seat. Pulling his cap brim down over his face, Trace closed his eyes. Instead of sleeping, he concentrated on the Super Stock practice laps he had done at Headwaters Speedway . . .

"Start out slow. No rush. First you need to get the feel of the car," John Sitz shouted above the engine noise of his own yellow No. 29 Super Stock. From the cockpit, Trace nodded. He was strapped in, buckled down, ready to roll. Johnny Walters had opened the Headwaters Speedway track on a Monday morning just for Trace—so he could get ready for his Wednesday tryout in Grand Forks. Local racing people were like that, like family. If you needed something at the track—a tire, an air compressor, a socket wrench, a coil spring—or if you needed help off the track in order to be ready for race night, all you had to do was ask. Or not. As with a family, everybody who raced at Headwaters knew everything about everyone, and when word got around about Trace's tryout, John Sitz had stepped up to volunteer his Super Stock (he also raced Late Models) without being asked.

Trace feathered the accelerator and checked the gauges: red, blue, and green for oil pressure, water temperature, and fuel pressure.

"All good?" John called, leaning into the cockpit to look at the flat dashboard.

Trace nodded again, impatient to get going.

"Remember, you've got a lot more horsepower than that

Street Stock of yours," Sitz shouted, "but don't be afraid of it. Make it work for you. Trust the car."

Trace nodded, half listening. He wondered at what rpm his heart was beating.

"Take a few slow laps to get the feel of the steering and the setup, all right?"

Trace looked down pit row. He flexed his left leg. Sitz's clutch was strung way softer than he was used to. He brought up the rpm for a smooth start—then lurched forward and killed the engine.

John's laughter filled the suddenly quiet cockpit. "Don't worry about it. This beast has a hair trigger for a clutch."

Trace quickly restarted the engine and, with more rpm and a slower pedal release, eased forward down pit row. Idling along at a throaty rumble, Trace felt strange being the only driver, the only car in the pits; everything seemed larger, and farther away. Then again, Trace was glad there weren't any other spectators. He blipped the throttle—and the Chevy V-8 engine barked like a big dog on a short chain. Steering No. 29 to the entrance at turn 4, he rolled up over the embankment and down onto the track. In this car the dirt was way closer—as if he could reach down and touch it.

Crawling around the track at yellow-flag speed, No. 29 was a Thoroughbred racehorse itching to run. By contrast, Trace's Street Stock was an old workhorse. He damn well better make the new Super Stock team; it would be tough going back to his old car.

Johnny Walters, Mel's father and the track owner, sat on his ATV by the exit at turn 3. Trace's father and John Sitz stood next to him, leaning against the big bumper tires, with their arms crossed. As Trace came by on his first lap, his father did not, he was glad to see, give a thumbs-up or wave.

On the straightaway and then on the banked turn, Trace swerved the car left, right, left, as he tried to get a feel for the steering quickener, for the shock absorbers, for the tires. After Trace's fifth slow lap, John stepped forward and waggled his right pointer finger: a little faster.

Trace brought the speed up slightly, intermittently punching the accelerator, breaking loose the rear tires. The engine's throaty grunts echoed in the empty grandstand. The Super Stock wanted to run; it hated being held down. After a couple of laps at this pace, Trace's back muscles relaxed; his spine began to conform to the seat. He loosened his ten o'clock–two o'clock death grip on the steering wheel.

As Trace approached turn 3, John stepped forward and spun his pointer finger in a quick, tight circle: hot laps!

Trace cranked up the thunder. He took the car into the turn at what he guessed was three-quarters speed. No. 29 hugged the inside bank, then pitched itself out of the apex like a baseball curling out of a pitcher's hand. His old Street Stock leaned, tipped, and tilted through the turns. Most full-framed race cars were happy to be done with a turn and headed down the straightaway; this Super Stock loved the turns—couldn't get to them quick enough.

Trace pressed faster around the track. The more he trusted the car and the setup, the smoother—and faster—he felt. After several hot laps, John abruptly waved him into the pits. Trace turned off the track and killed the rumbling engine. He coasted to a stop.

"Okay," John said. "Looks like you're getting a feel for the car."

"Yeah. I love it," Trace said with a grin.

"Good," John said. "Ready to do some hot laps?"

Trace stared.

"What?" John asked.

"I thought those *were* hot laps."

"You were getting up to speed, kid," John said with a smile. "But you're gonna have to be a little quicker to be competitive. The important thing is to find a line that works for you. High, low, medium—you be the judge. Take only what the track conditions give you. One night a track will be a dry slick, and the next night it will be rubbered up from lots of water. You've got to *feel* what's underneath your tires, *feel* where the best bite is."

"Got it," Trace said.

"But the key thing to driving a Super Stock or a Late Model is this: Never drive too deep into a turn. Then you'll have to use the brakes, because that's how we all drive normally off the track. On the track, in each corner you've got to find your lift point—when you lift off the gas. Then your goal is to accelerate *through* the turn. You'll have way more control that way."

Trace nodded.

"Now get back out there," John said, slapping Trace upside the helmet, "and drive this sucker like it was stolen."

Trace fired the engine, spun the tires, and surged back onto the track.

Coming out of turn 4, he threw the hammer down. The empty grandstand flashed by on his right—and turn 1 came up fast. Trace resisted the instinct to tap the brake. Rather, he let off the gas sooner than with his Street Stock—then pitched hard into the turn and cranked the steering wheel to the left. The Super Stock swung its rear end wide right. Trace got back on the throttle in a thundering, tire-spinning drift. G-forces pinned him to the right side of his shoulder harness as the car surged left—and out through the turn into the straightaway. "Sweet!" he shouted. But there was no time to celebrate; turn 2 loomed in his visor. Again he threw the car sideways into the high bank, and again No. 29 slung itself through the corner. It was like the tires had claws, and the car had wings . . .

"Trace. Trace—wake up! We're almost there."

Trace lurched upright in his seat. He couldn't believe it: he had actually fallen asleep for a few minutes. His heartbeat punched up a new rhythm. A bunch of tall grain elevators marked the east side of the city—that and the sudden, rank smell of a sugar beet plant.

"Gross," Trace said, wrinkling his nose.

"That's the smell of money," replied Trace's dad, a businessman farmer who knew about such things.

As they crossed the Red River bridge and entered North Dakota, Trace glanced behind. Their little Headwaters Speedway convoy was intact. They passed a few stoplights, crossed the railroad tracks, then made a right turn toward Rivers Speedway. When he wasn't racing, Trace came here once or twice each summer to watch sprint car races. On those occasions he passed through the old stone archway with the other race fans. Today his father headed around the back side, to the pit area. Grasshoppers began to hop and flutter inside Trace's stomach.

The empty parking lot, the silent grandstand—it was like nobody was here. Even the trailer park just across the fence was quiet.

"It was Wednesday, right?" his father asked.

"Yes. The last day of July," Trace said immediately. Then he pointed. Ahead near the pit gate was a youngish black woman talking on a cell phone; she held a clipboard. They drove forward. TEAM BLU SUPER STOCK TRYOUTS read a small sign taped to the chain-link gate behind her. In the background, at slow speed, a Super Stock crawled around the track.

Trace's father stopped at the pit gate and powered down the window.

"Hold on," the woman said into her phone. She looked at Trace's father, then at Trace. "Name?"

"Trace Bonham," Don said.

She glanced at her list, then checked off Trace's name. "Gotcha. Straight on through to the pit," she said with a nice smile. Then she looked at the other cars close behind. "This your entourage?"

"I'm afraid so," Don said.

"Okay, but they can't be in the tryout area. They'll have to sit in the stands," she said, "and no photos of any kind."

"No problem," Don said. Trace was already texting Mel.

"Go on in, then," the girl said, waving them forward. "And good luck."

If little old Headwaters Speedway felt empty during Trace's practice laps, the big Rivers Speedway pit area was a ghost town. No large car haulers. No motor coaches. No long, parallel rows of tractor-trailer rigs squeezed in an arm's length apart. No humming choir of generators. No smells of freshly ground tire rubber, racing fuel, popcorn, and barbecued ribs. No speeding ATVs with stressed-out track officials talking into headsets.

"Up there," Trace said, and pointed. A small cluster of vehicles and people had gathered at the far end, near turn 3. A big motor home with darkly tinted windows sat nearby, along with Cal Hopkins's long No. 42 trailer.

As they approached, faces turned to look. Several sets of fathers and sons, and at least one teenage girl and her dad, stared at the shiny Bonham Chevy. The kids all wore racing suits, tops down and sleeves tied at waist in hot weather, pre-race style.

"I told you, you should have worn your suit," his dad said.

"Don't worry, I'll put it on!" Trace replied.

His dad parked. They got out and walked forward, Trace leading the way. Walk too slow and he'd look timid. Walk too fast and he'd look anxious. Above all, don't look at the competition. But in the end, tryouts were the same everywhere: a bunch of kids standing around, sizing one another up while trying not to be obvious. Here, some yawned and pretended to be bored. Others talked and laughed too loudly. A couple of fathers murmured instructions into their kids' ears, a useless task because each kid was thinking the same thing: *Who looks quickest? Oldest? Strongest? Who has just the right gear?*

This group of teenagers all wore multilayer fire-retardant racing suits. Simpson. ProTech. The suits were well-worn, their colors faded and oil-spotted—which didn't necessarily mean that the kids had been racing for years. Young drivers often wore their dads' old racing suits, altered to fit. The used suits made them look fast just standing still. Nobody would be caught dead wearing brand-new gear.

"Name?" a woman in sunglasses said to Trace.

Trace opened his mouth. His voice croaked and cracked. Quickly he cleared his throat. "Trace Bonham." No one laughed, though from the side he saw a couple of kids look at their shoes.

"You race at Headwaters Speedway over in Minnesota, right?" the woman asked, looking at her clipboard. She wore red lipstick and had zero tan.

"That's right."

One of the loud-talking kids whispered something to another driver.

"Do they wear racing suits over there?" the woman asked.

"Yes, ma'am." There were a couple of chuckles this time, including a smile from the lone girl driver.

"Well, get yours on," the woman said. "We're almost ready to start."

Trace went back to the Tahoe and quickly changed. His father stayed with the group, where the pale-faced woman with the clipboard flipped open her phone. Her lips moved really fast. Trace zipped his suit and grabbed his helmet. As he exited the Tahoe, three more black-dressed people came out of the big motor home. They all carried cameras.

"All right," the lead woman said, "we're pretty much ready. My name is Laura Williams. I represent Team Blu, and I'm in charge here." Her voice, her accent, was not Minnesota or even midwestern—more like East Coast.

"Let's be totally clear on what we're doing today," she continued. "Because of your racing success and your age, you have been invited to try out for Team Blu, which is looking for a young driver—the right young driver."

Her camera-carrying assistants did not look from the Midwest, either. Who wore dark clothes in the middle of the day in July in North Dakota? Plus, they had odd haircuts—the style chopped or else spiky—and their sunglasses had frames unlike anything Trace had ever seen. The girl at the pit gate seemed like the most normal one on the team.

"My goal today is to get a good idea of who in this group is competitive in our driver search," Laura said. "But nothing will be decided today. The first order of business is to see you drive." She turned to the track, where an unmarked Super Stock powered up for a thundering hot lap. As the car surged close past the fence, the woman and her assistants flinched and covered their ears. Trace and the other young drivers watched without moving or changing expressions.

As the Super Stock slowed toward the pits, Laura looked back to her notes. "Each of you will get four warm-up laps, then two hot laps. And while your lap times are important, they are not necessarily the determining factor in who wins this 'ride,' as you call it."

Several of the young drivers glanced sideways at one another.

"Questions?" Laura asked sharply.

There was silence. Then a short, stocky kid with big arms raised a hand. "You mean, the fastest lap times ain't the most important thing?" The kid had a faint drawl, possibly southern Iowa, in his voice.

"Aren't," Laura said impatiently. "And that's not what I said. Lap times are important for everybody, but there are other factors in today's screening process—like good grammar."

The Iowa kid's face reddened. His head pulled down onto

his shoulders like a turtle's drawing back into its shell. The rest of the teenage drivers remained expressionless.

"In addition to time trials, each of you will do an interview as well as a photo shoot," Laura continued.

There was silence among the group of drivers; their eyes went to the assistants and their cameras, then to the motor home.

"Any more questions?" the woman asked.

The silence continued. Then the girl driver spoke up. "Who is Team Blu, anyway?" she asked. "I mean, it's the sponsor, right?"

"That's right," Laura said.

"Sponsors have products, like gas or oil or pizzas or whatever. What does Team Blu sell?" The girl had short brown hair, and brown eyes to match.

"Our product is not important at the moment," the woman said. "What's important is that we stay on schedule. We'll draw for the driving order."

There was nothing like a placement drawing to get drivers in motion, and Trace jostled his way into line. As he waited to draw, he found himself behind the Iowa kid, whose suit smelled like an open jar of pickles. Too many hot race nights in corn and hog country, not enough soap and water.

"There's something strange about this whole Team Blu thing," Trace murmured.

The kid shrugged, his small blue eyes focused on the drivers ahead. "Who cares? A ride's a ride."